NATUREWATCH

Also by Adrienne Katz
A WORLD IN YOUR KITCHEN

NATUREWATCH

Exploring nature with your children

ADRIENNE KATZ

Illustrated by Bridget Lewer

Addison-Wesley Publishing Company, Inc.

Reading, Massachusetts • Menlo Park, California • New York
Don Mills, Ontario • Wokingham, England • Amsterdam • Bonn
Sydney • Singapore • Tokyo • Madrid • San Juan

To Liane and Louise

Library of Congress Cataloging-in-Publication Data

Katz, Adrienne.
  Naturewatch : exploring nature with your children.

  Includes index.
  1. Natural history—Juvenile literature.   2. Nature study—
Juvenile literature.   I. Lewer, Bridget.
II. Title.
QH48.K25 1986   508   85-22968
ISBN 0-201-10457-1

Originally published in Britain in 1985
by Judy Piatkus (Publishers) Limited, London

First published in the U.S. in 1986 by
Addison-Wesley Publishing Company, Inc.

Illustrated by Bridget Lewer
Edited by Michael Johnstone
Designed by Zena Flax
Typeset by Tradespools Ltd., Frome, Somerset

     EFGHII-AL-89
Fifth printing, October 1989

CONTENTS

The author's rooftop garden

INTRODUCTION

Yonder see the morning blink,
The sun is up and up must I,
To wash and dress and eat and drink,
And look at things and talk and think.

Last poems A. E. Housman

The world around us is a fascinating place. To teach a child to open his eyes and mind to what is happening around him is to give him a gift for life.

You don't have to be a Picasso to appreciate beauty, or James Crockett to enjoy growing your own tiny patch of seeds from a supermarket packet, but you do need to be aware and observant if you are not to miss out on the details that make up the patchwork of life.

Sharing the world with a new, unspoilt mind, a person fresh to every sight and smell, is invigorating for grown-ups. You won't need to set aside great chunks of time – something all busy parents find hard to do – nor will you need any particular skills. All you need is interest and observation.

Perhaps when walking a child to school, leaves or cones might catch your eye. Pick them up and look at the way they are built. Marvel at the veins in the leaves; take the cones home and study and decorate them together. Stop and look at the way in which a spider's web is constructed. The world is full of wonders for high-rise dwellers and gardeners alike. The ideas set out here rely on the most familiar sights which seem so obvious that we take them for granted.

With the increase in the numbers of families living in cities, countless children are in danger of growing up without any involvement with plants, insects or mud pies. Making contact with nature is essential if youngsters are not to see this world as one of computer games and push-button slaves in a concrete and glass landscape.

Fragile butterflies, wriggling worms, birds, ants and bees are easily watched wherever you live. Plants can be grown inside or out, in sweeping gardens and in saucers.

The projects suggested here are intended to build up an awareness of what is going on all around us. Gradually, as the child's interest develops, whether in growing plants, arranging flowers, crafts or insect and bird life, you will find as we did, how one thing leads to another. Interdependent life cycles and food chains seemed to draw us into new questions. If the child sets the pace, his or her degree of curiosity leads you on in a relaxed way.

Before you embark on this odyssey, I must admit to weird and wonderful problems resulting from the love of plants in our family: the trees in the living room and dining area have reached the ceiling: the plant in the kitchen window has taken over every inch of space; and we have covered the entire roof area of our house with a garden. When plants are trailing down bannisters and entwining themselves around the coat stand, what then?

May I wish you the best of luck as you and your children explore the wonderful world of nature.

A note about using this book

This book has been written for both the adult and the child. In the light print I am talking to the adult, and alongside are boxed projects in a heavier type for children.

And now to all those girls reading this book – my apologies for using 'he' throughout when talking of the child. 'He' is a much used form, and turned out much less clumsy than 'he/she' or 'he or she', but I hope you will simply read 'he' as 'she' where necessary.

American readers will forgive the few Britishisms remaining in the text, and my thanks go to Roger Swain for translating it into American.

GROWING

AWARE

'... I was fascinated by water, I remember, and I would sit on the bank and stare at it for as long as people would let me, just looking into it and trying to imagine what it would be like to move in and out of the rocks, to have a concealed place somewhere in a dark cave deep away from the light.'

Pool in the Park Paddy Kinsale

SIMPLE JOYS

Very often, the things that jaded adults take for granted are sources of endless pleasure for children. When rain threatens, we reach for our umbrellas and raincoats, forgetting the pure joy of turning faces skywards to feel the raindrops on our faces. We desperately avoid puddles; they mischievously splash through them. We inwardly moan as we sweep autumn leaves off lawns or unblock drainpipes, but the inner child in us can't resist the temptation to scatter neatly piled leaves with one carefree kick. How refreshing to let that 'inner child' free once in a while — of course it's in a good cause, teaching a child about the world is all the justification you need!

WATER AND AWARENESS

Water may mean life to the plants, but it means joy to children. Pouring water from one container to the other, dripping, spurting and splashing with watering cans, buckets and funnels can keep toddlers happy for ages. But never allow your child to splash around in water more than a couple of inches deep: tragedies can occur in the shallowest stretches. Older children build dams or waterfalls, experiment and discover the way water behaves and are enchanted by rainbows in the arc of a sprinkler.

Let them strip off their clothes and run under the hosepipe spray on a hot summer's day, or take them into the park and let them splash around in the fountain. It's curious how even the stoniest hearted park-keeper smiles indulgently at the sight and sounds of toddlers dodging the shimmering streams of water.

Then let them lie still, drying off in the sun and watch the birds play under the drops, hopping away and returning again and again.

Now may be the time to talk about the ceaseless interaction between the surface of the land and water, and the lower layers of the air that covers them both. Explain that water is being sucked up, evaporating into the air then falling back to earth as rain or dew.

This can lead on to explaining about oxygen and carbon dioxide passing in and out of the bodies of living things. Gases leave the air to be dissolved in the ocean and then slowly leave the water to join the air again. The questions that these natural cycles may trigger off will lead you to search frantically for the family encyclopedia: it's not just your child who is learning.

WATER REPELLENT LEAVES

Look at a leaf and notice the way it repels water. Some are waxy and the water runs off, barely leaving a trace; others are furry and have little hairs to push the water off. The crystal droplets glisten like diamonds on the silvery leaves. Lamb's ears (Stachys byzantina) have these strokeable furry leaves. Water droplets on nasturtium leaves are round and plump, like drops of mercury.

Gather several different leaves and spray a little water on each: you will find several different water patterns. Some plants will channel the water to the ground along leaves that act as funnels or aqueducts. Can you find some that collect water in vase-shaped containers?

ON YOUR BACK LOOKING UP

Lie on your back and stare up at the clouds. There are games to play imagining the shapes of animals chasing each other across the sky, and then shifting and changing form, billowing and retreating all the time. Clouds are water, too. On a windy day when the clouds are scudding across the sky, try and imagine that they are still and that it is the buildings and trees that are racing past.

Lying on the ground is a feeling. Feel how the earth supports your body at various points, gently but firmly pressing against your shoulder-blades and heels, back and calves. Slowly, as you let go, it seems to be holding you up – do you feel the earth spinning a little? Trees look so different from here, birds zoom overhead, buildings loom dangerously. Buzzing and birdsong, a gentle hum reveals the activities going on around you.

Now close your eyes and listen to the sounds around you. How many can you positively identify? Which bird is that singing in the trees? Is that a bee or a wasp humming and buzzing by? Listen to the water dripping and the wind rustling the leaves. Can you hear your blood thudding in your ears and your heart beating? There are so many sounds to listen for, and they vary greatly as the seasons change.

Then clasp your hands over your ears and blot out sight and sound. Concentrate on what you can smell. Has the grass been recently cut? Can you smell the evening scents? Are there some sweet-smelling herbs nearby?

FUN WITH SAND

Remember letting sand run through your fingers, or the simple satisfaction of pouring it through a funnel? Those of us who had sandpits or were taken on beach holidays as children can recapture the feeling with instant recall.

Let a small child find out through play. If you can provide a corner with some clean sand (a plastic tub will do) watch your child wonder, 'Will the sand stay up in a mountain or fall again in a soft dune?' 'What will happen if I pour it through my fingers?' Pouring, making trails and wriggling toes, they are all there in a simple bag of sand. Wet the sand slightly and, as he builds his mud pies and sandcastles, memories of your own childhood will come flooding back to you.

Many children will make complicated road systems, with tunnels and flyovers looking like a futuristic science-fiction film location.

One word of warning! Remember to cover the sand with a strong lid at night so that cats do not avail themselves.

WINTER WONDERLAND

One night, at bedtime, the world is a dark, grim, grey place. The next morning it's been transformed into a glittering, white paradise. The branches of the trees are weighed down with shining snow and the bare rose bushes look as if they've been sprayed with frosty sugar.

Play games out there together. Listen to the crispy snow crunching under your feet. Look out for animal tracks imprinted on the white carpet. Find a slope together and pack the snow hard so that your children can slide down and feel the cold fresh air running through their hair. Who can resist making snowballs or building a towering snowman? Look closely at the snow crystals and see them glisten in the sunshine.

Winter is the king of showmen,
Turning tree stumps into snow men
And houses into birthday cakes
And spreading sugar over the lakes
Smooth and clean and frost white
The world looks good enough to bite.
That's the season to be young.
Catching snowflakes on your tongue.

Snow is snowy when it's snowing
I'm sorry it's slushy when it's going.

Winter Morning Ogden Nash

A CLOSER LOOK AT PLANTS

'O Tiger-lily,' said Alice, addressing herself
to one that was waving gracefully about in
the wind, 'I wish *you* could talk.'
  'We can talk,' said Tiger-lily, 'when
there's anybody worth talking to.'

Alice Through the Looking Glass Lewis Carroll

WHAT'S THAT?

When you have a toddler constantly beside you, the habit of pointing out and labelling objects as you see them is second nature. At some stage we all grab hold of a perfect flower, and, directing the child's attention to its scented loveliness, say the word 'flower'. To explain more about plant life is only to do more of the same.

Faced with the purity of the child's experience it seems as though you are writing on a blank page. The toddler grows into an inquiring child, asking, touching and wanting to know more about everything.

Take a flower apart gently, let your child touch it. He'll see the pollen come off on his fingers and notice how some petals are so velvety. Look together at the way the flowers are assembled on the stem – are they in clusters or arranged singly? Then there are those on a stem of their own waving in stately splendour.

As your child grows and he becomes more and more involved in what is happening around him, the level of showing and naming simply becomes more complex as you investigate the intricate network of plant life together.

'What's that?' soon becomes 'But how?', 'But why?' or 'When?' Answer at once if you can, but as you can't bluff kids – they have an uncanny knack of knowing when their parents are uncertain – try to discover the answer together.

BURSTING INTO BLOOM

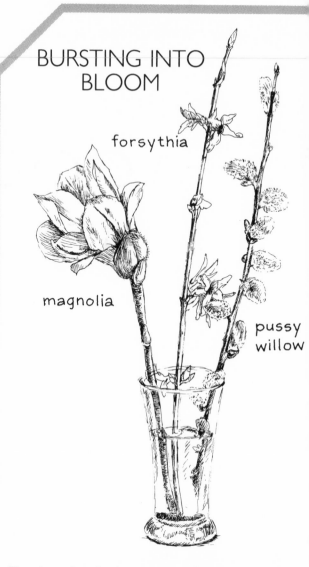

forsythia

magnolia

pussy willow

To take a close look at spring unfurling, put a few twigs with buds into a vase of water where you can see them easily. Forsythia will break dramatically into bloom; weeping willow stems will soon burst with leaves; pussy willow will turn from smooth silver curves to yellow fluff. Remember that a single daffodil in a jar can be more clearly watched as it opens than a bunch of them.

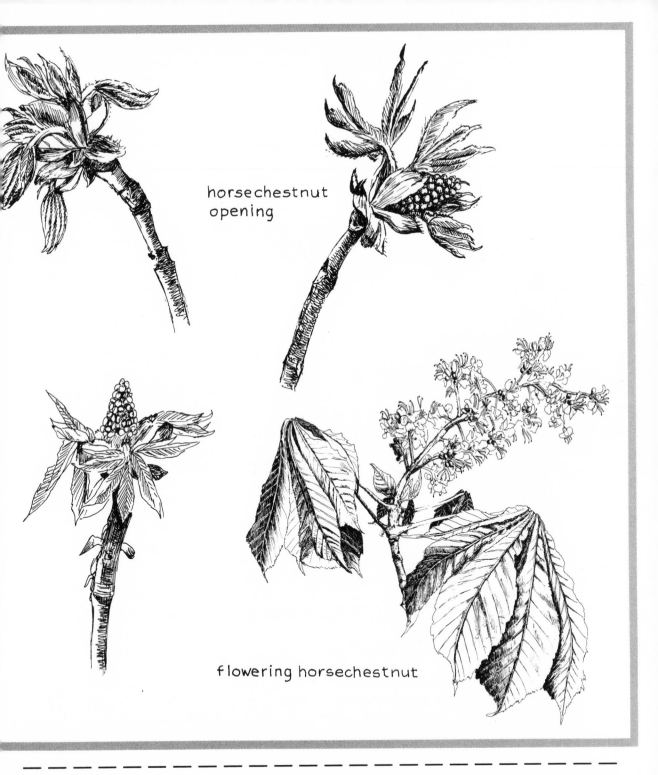

horsechestnut
opening

flowering horsechestnut

FROM
TINY SEEDS...

To understand the different stages of development between the planting of a seed and the production of new seeds for the next generation, your child will need to see the whole picture. This is easily done if you grow a hardy annual.

Choose some seeds that can be planted in spring. If

you follow the instructions on the back of the seed packet carefully, growth will be quick and the flowering showy. Together you can see how cleverly the flowers, with their colour and scent, attract the bees to the nectaries so that they must force their way into the flower, picking up pollen from the stamens in the process, and carrying it away to another flower where they deposit the pollen on the stigma. The flowers are brightly coloured and strongly scented not simply for our enjoyment, but to attract the pollinators to them.

Male cells in the pollen then join with female cells in the ovary. The pollen grain germinates to form a thin tube which forces its way into the ovule, fusing with the female cell which is now fertilized and grows into a new seed. The whole cycle is complete.

When there are dead heads on plants, don't snip them off: let them dry on the stem so that your child can see how the seed pods form after the petals fall.

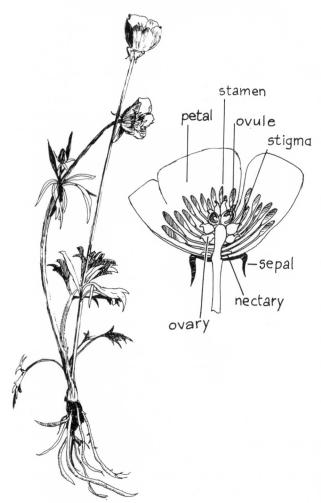

petal

stamen

ovule

stigma

sepal

nectary

ovary

WHY DO WE
WATER PLANTS?

One little boy thought I had a cleanliness mania because he was convinced that every day I was 'washing the bush to make it clean'! He was unaware that plants need water in order to survive and, being sure that you don't have to be clean to live, he knew that I was mad.

This tale illustrates how necessary it is to explain what seems to us either self-evident or so basic as not to need demonstration.

'What do plants do with water?'
They drink it!

To show this to your child, place the stem of Busy Lizzie (*Impatiens*) in a jar half-filled with water. Seal the mouth of the jar with Plasticine or Playdough, firming it

around the stem. Mark the level of water in the jar.

Watch the level go down rapidly over a couple of days and await the next question.

'But where does the water go to?'

To demonstrate the answer to this you'll need a pot plant and a plastic bag with a tie. Place the bag over the plant and tie it securely at the base of the stem. Water evaporating from the leaves will soon condense inside the plastic, and when the droplets become heavy they will run down and drop like rain on the plant below.

'Where does the water go to?' The plants transpire ... OK, they sweat, only instead of pores on the skin as we have, they have stomata on leaves which open when light falls on them and the moisture escapes into the warm dry air.

PLANTS NEED LIGHT, WARMTH AND WATER

When plants draw up water from the soil they also take in nutrients which they use to manufacture their own food, using sunlight, by a process called photosynthesis. Sap is the lifeblood of the plant and carries the nutrients to the leaves where the photosynthesis takes place.

We depend on plants, because they use carbon dioxide, and give off oxygen (see page 27).

(see page 27)

MAKE A FLOWER BLUSH

Would you like to see the route of water through the plant?

Colour some water with some red ink or vegetable dye and stand a daisy in it.

The dye will gradually be sucked up through the plant and the flower will gradually take on a red tint. The little vessels carrying the fluid will be clearly marked by the dye.

Try this with a fleshy thick-stemmed geranium cutting and then slice up the stem to have a look at a cross-section both vertically and horizontally, as in the drawing.

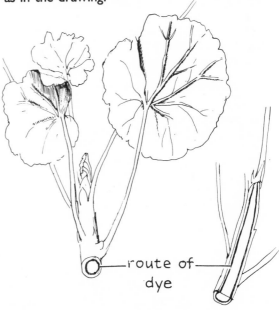

route of dye

Look at a few leaves to trace their veins. Where a leaf was joined to the stem, you will be able to find the marks of the veins, usually noticeable as little holes. Count the number of these holes and the number of main veins on the leaves. You will find the same number of little holes in leaf and stem, marking their junction.

FIND OUT
WHAT PLANTS NEED

Pot four identical plants in pots of the same size, and in the same mixture.

Give one plant ample water, light and warmth. Give the second one water and warmth, but no light, the third water and light but no warmth and the fourth light and warmth but no water.

Compare your results.

The one without water will shrivel and die.

The one with no warmth will hardly thrive.

The plant with no light will be lanky and pale.

The one with all three, light, warmth and water, will be green and sturdy, healthy and flourishing.

WATCH IT GROW

Growth seems more remarkable when you can actually see it. Changes happening in measurable terms are more exciting for children than simply talking about it.

Try to grow a plant where you and your child can watch it at frequent intervals, on a window sill or kitchen table. Impatient children will be rewarded by the speedy growth of many of these suggested experiments.

MUSTARD AND CRESS

Any shallow container in the kitchen can be used as a growing bed for mustard or cress if lined with blotting paper or kitchen towel. A colander is best, but an empty plastic margarine tub with some holes stabbed in the bottom is just as good. Sow the cress three days before the mustard if you intend to harvest them

SPROUTING

Put a few butterbeans between two layers of damp cottonwool on a saucer. (No. You're not building them a little nest: the cottonwool holds the water well.)

Watch the seeds germinate and sprout as they swell and burst. Shoots emerge and you can see how they always grow upward whatever angle the beans are set, while the roots always grow downward. Move them around and they still grow this way.

Really fast growth can be seen if you line a glass jar with dampened blotting paper and put sunflower, corn, peas, beans or radish seeds between the glass and the paper. This way, you get a perfect view of the developing seeds.

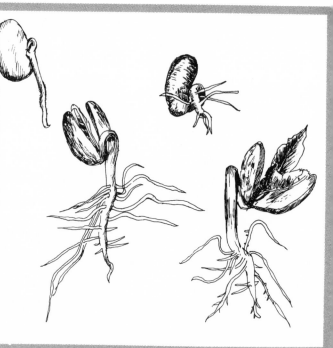

together. Cover with a sheet of paper for the first few days. Harvest ten days after sowing. They need to be rinsed frequently with fresh water or they become smelly, that's what the holes are for. Your child can do this as often as he wishes – at least once a day.

GROWING FROM LEFTOVERS

potato sprouting

carrot top

Before you throw away the tops of carrots, parsnips or pineapples, set them aside. These will make good subjects for visible growth.

Many fruits and vegetables will produce shoots. Try swedes, beetroot, turnip and, of course, potatoes.

Let your child grow them in a shallow container with a little water in it, and you'll soon have a jungle on your windowsill.

Cut the carrot or other root vegetable with an inch (2·5 cm) of flesh remaining at the top; the shoots will sprout from the top. Pineapples will produce rosettes of prickly leaves quite easily by this method.

GROWING BULBS IN WATER

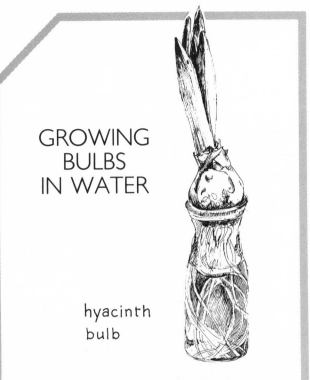

hyacinth bulb

Certain narcissi, the paperwhites, are so easy to grow, needing no soil, but only a few pebbles or gravel to hold the bulbs steady. This means that you will be able to see the root growth between the pebbles. Crocuses, too, will grow easily in pebbles or in a bulb glass. Hyacinths are best of all. The sight of a hyacinth grown in water in a bulb glass or even a jam jar, is quite dramatic.

Place the hyacinth bulb in a jar filled with water and put it in a cool dark place for eight weeks. The bulb should be just above the water level. Visit them occasionally and watch how the roots develop and the shoots emerge, all pale and blanched.

When you bring the glass out into the light these shoots should be about 2·5 cm (an inch) high, and the roots will have formed a bundle of silvery white strings. Keep them in a cool but light place and the peculiar looking onion-like bulb will quickly produce large, strongly scented flowers.

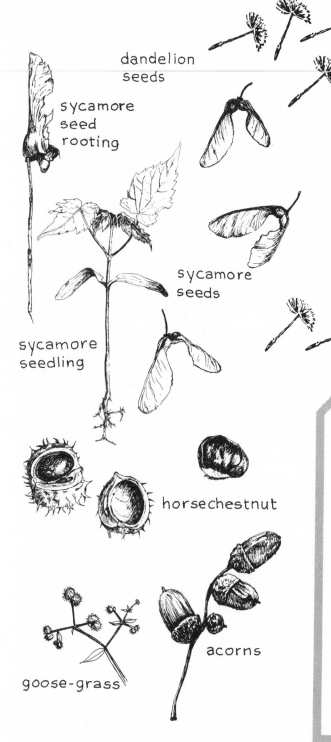

dandelion
seeds

sycamore
seed
rooting

sycamore
seeds

sycamore
seedling

horsechestnut

goose-grass

acorns

SEENS: *SEEDS:*
HERE, THERE AND
EVERYWHERE

When you stop and think about it, there are seeds in various forms everywhere. From tomato pips to date stones, the world is full of seeds.

If the mud is scraped from a child's boots and carefully mixed with compost, a variety of plants will grow which will demonstrate how clever plants are at spreading their seeds.

Nature has designed ingenious methods for plants to disperse their seeds. Thistle and dandelion seeds are

GROW YOUR OWN

Have you ever thought of growing dried peas or lentils? Place a piece of dried canvas over a soil-filled seed box. Spread the seeds over the canvas and cover with the flap. Put a larger box over the whole lot and keep it out of the light.

Be patient, and within a few weeks they will germinate – a tiny root will break through the case of the seed and a few days later a little shoot will appear.

Apple pips take longer, but they can be germinated by putting the pips between two layers of cottonwool in a jar in the fridge.

You can germinate bird seed, hamster seed-mix ... any seed in fact, although some take quite a while.

An acorn will shoot if you first wrap it in damp cottonwool and put it in a plastic bag. When the shoot emerges, plant it in a pot. Your great-grandchildren may be able to sit in the shade of a mighty oak tree that began life in your plastic bag.

borne on the wind on little parachutes. Burrs of burdock attach seeds to the coats of passing animals. Mallow pods simply burst open, spraying seeds onto the ground, and ash seeds fly on fragile paper wings. The seeds of some fruits and berries that are eaten by birds are passed out through their digestive systems and take root far from the parent plant.

The fruit of the harebell produces a pepperpot type of seed spreader, while many people call that of the cowslip the salt pot. Sycamore and maple seeds travel on key-shaped wings, while ash and lime travel on twisted wings.

Poppies burst open dramatically and scatter their seeds all around. And when the seeds are settled, they send down roots and little shoots grow upwards. The seeds become plants which in turn produce seeds...

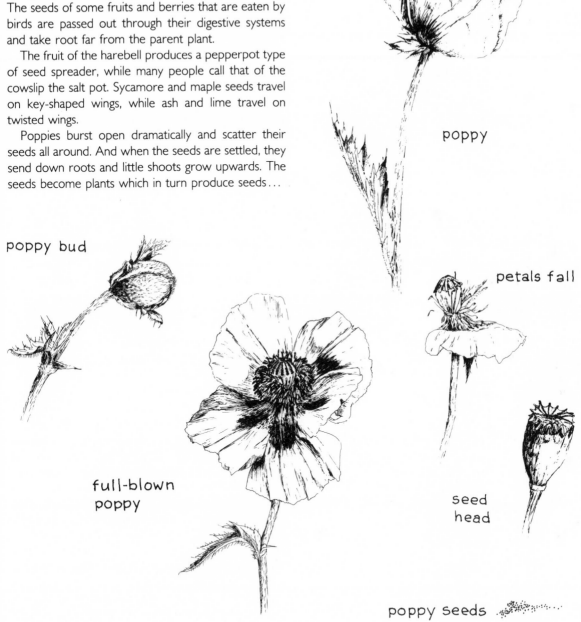

poppy

poppy bud

petals fall

full-blown poppy

seed head

poppy seeds

NEW PLANTS FROM OLD

spider plant

Is there a way to form new plants without growing them from seed? Try these methods.

The ease with which you can make 'babies' or 'chicks' with spider plants or 'hen-and-chicks' (*chlorophytum*) makes them a favourite with children. The new plantlets are produced on runners which cascade out of the central rosette of leaves. These can be rooted in the same pot if it is large enough, keeping the runners intact until the babies are well-established. Or they can be rooted in another pot, again keeping the runner intact until the chicks have developed their own root systems and can be cut off from the main plant.

The same can be done with mother-of-thousands (*Saxifraga stolonifera*), or pick-a-back plants (*Tolmiea menziesii*) which produce runners with plantlets and also form new plantlets at the base of their downy leaves.

These plants are ideal for children. They can multiply them, producing new plants to give as gifts, or simply let the 'babies' remain decoratively on the parent plant.

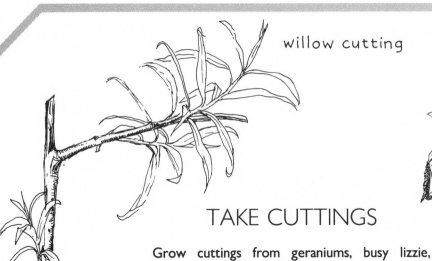

willow cutting

TAKE CUTTINGS

busy lizzie rooting in jam jar

Grow cuttings from geraniums, busy lizzie, cactus, carnations, privet, currant, fuchsias, santpaulias and, of course, a branch from a weeping willow.

Leave your cuttings – busy lizzies and willow are quickest – in a glass of water on an inside window ledge. Trim some leaves off in an effort to minimize loss of water by transpiration and wait for the roots to form. When they have appeared and are growing well, put the cutting in a pot with a layer of pebbles or broken pots at the bottom to allow for drainage, and firm the potting compost around it.

Fuchsia cuttings do best if they're placed in a pot of sharp sand and covered with the inverted lower half of a plastic cold-drinks bottle that has been cut in two. This creates a mini-greenhouse that traps the evaporating moisture and keeps your little plant damp.

Many plants can be propagated by *layering* a stem on the ground. To do this, weigh a stem down gently by tying a light weight to the end – heavy enough to keep part of the stem in contact with the ground, but not too heavy to break it. Where the stem remains in contact with the ground, new roots will develop which can be cut off and planted. Some plants can be pegged down, but others are so delicate that a hairpin is enough to keep them in touch with the earth.

ON THE MOVE

One of the many strange things about plants is the bending movements that they make in response to light, gravity and water. Children are intrigued by these movements, called tropisms, enjoying the experiments you do together to observe them. Once interested, there are projects that they can do for themselves.

When a plant receives light from one side only, it will bend towards the source of light. Plants grown on your windowsill with the light coming from one side only will need regular turning if they are to grow straight. My sweetpea seedlings, forgotten on the windowsill for two days, leant heavily in a neat column rather like the leaning tower of Pisa.

Another example of plant movement or response is when seeds are planted at random angles. They sort themselves out, sending shoots heavenwards and roots earthwards.

sunflower seedlings growing towards the light

BEND TO THE LIGHT

In grass shoots, such as wheat or oats, growth is stimulated by a hormone called auxin which is produced at the tip of the shoot. Auxin causes the cells here to grow longer. The production of the hormone is inhibited by light.

When the tip of the shoot points towards the light, it grows straight because it receives equal amounts of light on all sides.

If light comes from one side only, there is less cell elongation on that side and therefore less growth. The cells on the other side will grow longer and faster, causing the shoot to bend over towards the source of light.

The word heliotropism comes from two Greek words, *helios*, meaning sun, and *tropos* meaning turn. As the plants will respond to any light source, not necessarily sunlight, and the Greek word for light is *photo*, the more technically correct term for the phenomenon is *phototropism*.

GROWING AT LIGHT ANGLES

To see how plants grow towards light, pot up two seedlings and find two cardboard boxes, large enough to cover the pots. Cut a small slit two-thirds of the way up each box. Put one plant in each box: light will reach the plants through the slits.

Put one box to one side and leave it. Lift the other box slightly each day and turn the plant 45°.

After a week remove both boxes.

The plant that has not been turned will have bent towards the light. The one that was evenly exposed to the light will have grown straight upwards, showing how the light influences the direction of plant growth. This is called *heliotropism*.

A QUESTION OF SOME GRAVITY

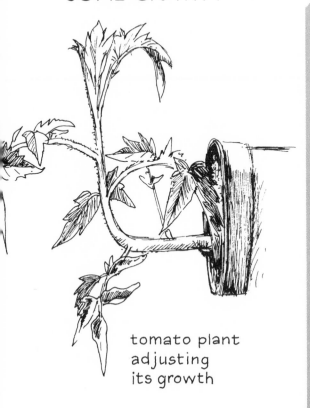

tomato plant
adjusting
its growth

As you explore the world of plants more fully, you will come across gravity and the way in which it affects growth movement. Its effect on plant growth can easily be demonstrated by laying seedlings or bean sprouts on their sides and leaving them for a day. Within 24 hours, the shoots and roots will have made a right-angled turn: the shoots will be growing skywards and the roots downwards.

In controlled experiments, two sets of plants are turned on their sides. If one set is turned regularly so as to be evenly exposed to gravity it will grow straight outwards, while the set that has not been turned adjusts itself to the new direction and changes the angle of growth, as in the case of the tomato plant above.

ROOTING AROUND IN THE DARK...

Watch how gravity affects roots by pinning a few pea or bean seeds to a cork and placing the cork in the mouth of a jar that has been lined with moist blotting paper or kitchen towel. Lay the jar on its side in a dark place for a few days. When you look at it next, the roots will be growing downwards, sensitive to the force of gravity.

beans pinned to cork

moist blotting paper
lining jar

... AND IN THE WET

Roots will also seek out water. To see this, place a small plant in the corner of a rectangular container filled with soil. Water regularly *but only in one spot*, the corner furthest away from your plant. After a week or two, the roots will be growing towards the moisture.

THE
POTATO OBSTACLE RACE

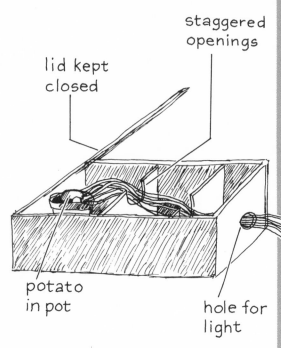

staggered openings

lid kept closed

potato in pot

hole for light

Stems are sensitive to light, and you can see this by constructing an experimental obstacle course for a potato.

Put a potato plant in a pot into a corner of a strong rectangular box. Make two partitions to go across the box, with an opening in each partition to allow the stems through. Insert the partitions but stagger the position of the openings by placing one to the left of the box and one to the right. Make a hole, 5 cm (2 inches) across, at the far end. Cover with a lid.

The potato stems will seek the light and twist their way around the partitions and out through the end hole. Green leaves will only form in the light.

STRANGE MOVEMENTS

Several plants, such as morning glory, close their flowers at night, and your child may well have noticed this. Look for other plants that move in odd ways.

The prayer plant (*Maranta leuconeura kerchoviana*) folds its leaves as if in prayer each evening.

Mimosa pudica withdraws and folds up its feathery leaves when touched: this sensitive plant straightens up again when the stimulus is removed.

There are several plants that move in order to eat. Has your child discovered that there are insect-eaters in the plant world?

Venus flytraps (*dionaea muscipula*) are insect eaters, catching their prey in jaw-like traps and digesting it with juices.

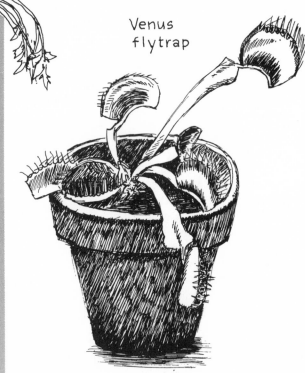

Venus flytrap

Pitcher plants *Sarracenia* and *Darlingtonia* have vase-shaped leaves containing a fluid in which insects drown and then dissolve – a science-fiction nightmare not for the faint-hearted.

Sundews (*Drosera rotundifolia*) trap insects in viscous 'dew drops' then fold hairs around them to hold the insects securely while digesting.

Butterworts (*Pinguicula alpina*) trap insects on their sticky leaves which then curl over them and secrete digestive juices over the prey.

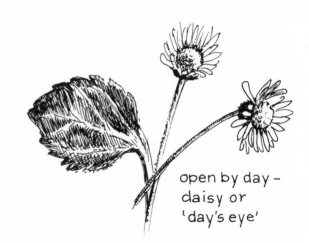

open by day – daisy or 'day's eye'

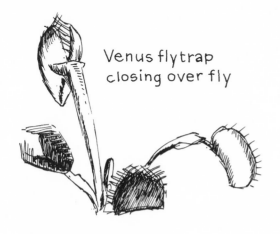

Venus flytrap closing over fly

SLEEPY HEADS

If your child has noticed that certain plants close their flowers in the afternoon or when the sun vanishes, you may have been asked 'Do the daisies go to sleep?' Well, in a sense they do. There are several reasons why certain plants do this. It may be to protect the delicate flowers from heat or glare, or because the pollinating insects are no longer around. Temperature and moisture also play their part.

Plants manufacture food using the sunlight to combine nutrients in the sap with carbon dioxide from the air, to form sugars and starches to feed themselves. When daylight fades, plants stop doing this. They give off oxygen. This process is photosynthesis. When the plant is manufacturing food its tissues are firmer than when it is giving off oxygen and moisture.

If your child is eager to get out of bed, he may well see the early risers, like crocuses. They open at dawn and go to bed in the afternoon. Goat's beard goes to sleep around mid-day, too (something many mothers wish their toddlers would do as well).

In the evening, go out together and look for flowers that go to sleep, closing when the sun goes down. Daisies on the lawn close, so do tulips and gazanias and water lillies on the pond. Wood sorrel will neatly fold up its leaves.

Interestingly, honeysuckle flowers open at night and give off a powerful scent to attract moths.

daisy closed at night

GETTING TO GRIPS

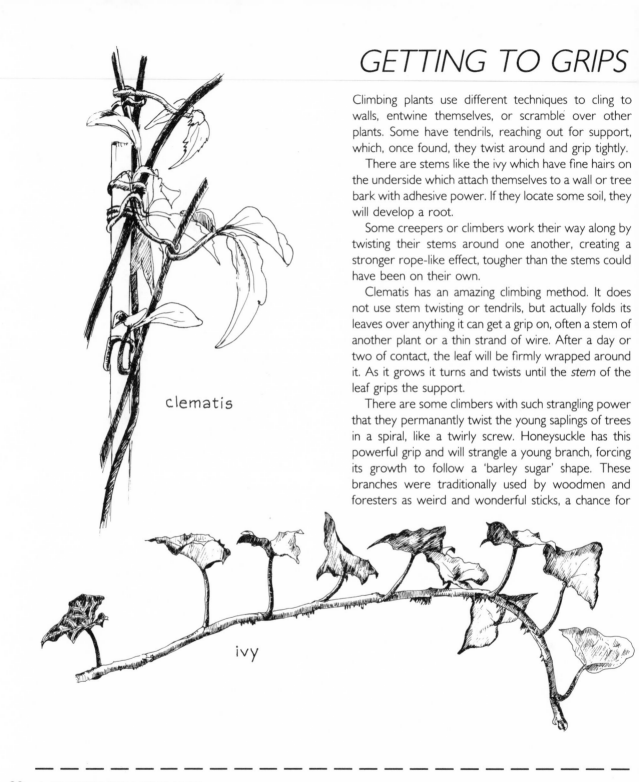

clematis

ivy

Climbing plants use different techniques to cling to walls, entwine themselves, or scramble over other plants. Some have tendrils, reaching out for support, which, once found, they twist around and grip tightly.

There are stems like the ivy which have fine hairs on the underside which attach themselves to a wall or tree bark with adhesive power. If they locate some soil, they will develop a root.

Some creepers or climbers work their way along by twisting their stems around one another, creating a stronger rope-like effect, tougher than the stems could have been on their own.

Clematis has an amazing climbing method. It does not use stem twisting or tendrils, but actually folds its leaves over anything it can get a grip on, often a stem of another plant or a thin strand of wire. After a day or two of contact, the leaf will be firmly wrapped around it. As it grows it turns and twists until the *stem* of the leaf grips the support.

There are some climbers with such strangling power that they permanantly twist the young saplings of trees in a spiral, like a twirly screw. Honeysuckle has this powerful grip and will strangle a young branch, forcing its growth to follow a 'barley sugar' shape. These branches were traditionally used by woodmen and foresters as weird and wonderful sticks, a chance for

honeysuckle
climbing
clockwise

a bramble
uses thorns
to grip

climbing
techniques of
sweet pea

users to be a little eccentric, and display a stick that no one else could rival.

On a woodland walk, keep an eye open for such a stick, and look for twisting plants. You will notice that black bryony grows clockwise, while bindweed twists anti-clockwise. Honeysuckle climbs up in a clock-wise spiral.

Coiling begins when the wind moves the plant and the tendrils rub against a support. This action stimulates growth on the other side, away from the chafing. This makes it twist round and grip. Once this happens, the remainder of the tendril (and often the spare ones next to it) will curl into a tight spiral.

JUST A WEED

dandelion

Dandelions, popping up in lawns, pathways, between stones and on gravel – waving their golden heads, take their name from their spreading jagged leaves. They are said to look like lion's teeth, in French *dents-de-lions*.

We always think of them as being yellow: an observant child may spot a white one in a sea of yellow. The flowers close at night, or during the day if the sun disappears behind dark clouds for a long time. To help your child see this in detail, put a bucket over a dandelion flower and it will gradually close up.

When the flower has been pollinated, it will also close up and hang its head, no need now to try to attract the insects.

Eventually, the flower petals will wither and fall, no longer needed. The seeds have been developing inside and now the plant prepares to disperse them. The flower heads straighten up and the seeds will be offered to the wind, equipped with their own feathery parachutes.

Break a stem in two, or tear a leaf, and you will see the white sap ooze out. This has been used to make a sort of rubber, but its real job is to feed the plant.

Anyone who has tried pulling up a dandelion, will have been surprised to realize how deep the roots go into the soil. These long roots enable the dandelion to grow between paving stones and other apparently soil-less spots. If you tear a plant out of its crack and do not remove the root, it will simply produce a new stem and flower.

SALAD DAYS

Dandelions are a favourite food of rabbits, guinea pigs and even goats. You can make a delicious salad with them, too.

To do this, keep the leaves entirely covered so that they are not exposed to any light. An upturned box, bucket or flowerpot will be ideal. After two or three weeks they will have turned white, lost their bitterness and be ready for eating after they have been washed.

LIFE ON A WALL

There's plenty of plant life to be spotted on an old wall. Drystone walls are those in which stones are fitted skilfully together without any mortar. There are crevices and crannies in all types of wall, and over a period of time soil gathers in these and begins to support plants. They force their roots into slits where the soil is kept moist in dark cracks.

Plants suited to rocky outcrops and cliff faces are happy on a wall that is dry as they need little moisture. Stonecrops are such plants, being able to store water in their fleshy leaves.

On a damp wall there will be ferns and mosses. The mosses have fine stalks on which there are little capsules. These release spores as fine dust that fly through the air and, in turn, settle in cracks of their own to develop into mosses themselves. There are also tiny ferns keeping a tenacious grip on life.

There is life on a wall all year round: maidenhair, spleenwort, rustyback fern, ivy-leafed toadflax, red valerian, navelwort and, of course, on the dry side of the wall, lichens, which can tell you a great deal about the pollution level of the air. These simple, rootless plants absorb rain-water and gases through the upper surfaces of their leaves and cannot exist in a polluted atmosphere. They are seldom seen in built-up areas, and as towns and cities spread, the lichen population is thought to be dwindling.

As well as plants, there is a host of insects that love basking on a sunny wall: and the little spiders living in these walls have an ideal home and a steady stream of food passing by.

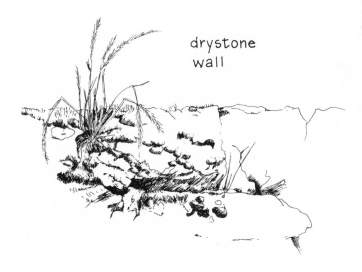

drystone wall

A GARDEN
OF YOUR OWN

'I've gotter garden. I've got Virginia Stock grow'n all over it. It grows up in no time. An' must'erd 'n cress grows in no time too. I like things what grow quick, don't you? You get tired of waiting for the other sorts, don't you?

William the Intruder Richmal Crompton

HAVING A GARDEN IS A STATE OF MIND

Having a garden involves more than mere ownership of the patch itself. It is to do with the actual growing of plants. Window box or rolling acres, gardening is tending plants and trying to create beauty in spite of weather, pests or space.

If you're stuck in a bus queue clutching a plant, true gardeners will talk to you – rambling on about their own specimens doing so well this year. They'll give you tips about this species' special tastes and Auntie Mabel's proven belief that such and such a plant must have tea leaves in spring. True gardeners are as emotionally tied to plants as mothers are to babies. Many will tell you how they talk to their plants to encourage or thank them: they're not nuts, they simply talk to their green acquaintances, as Rolf Harris says, 'like the friends they are.'

Some gardeners have experimented with music, and one Montreal plant-shop owner believes that plants particularly appreciate classical or oriental music. While I don't suggest that you hire a string quartet to play Brahms to your begonias, I am saying that human and plant life are interdependent.

You don't need vast fields to become a farmer and grow vegetables to harvest for your table. You don't need bulging borders to create a pretty flower arrangement.

Gardening itself brings many joys. Working with plants is food for the soul of an artistic child, growing edible plants provides food for a hungry one.

Lastly, and perhaps most important of all, it's a legitimate excuse to get messed up. I've seen children from high-rise homes touch the soil wonderingly and nervously at first – afraid of the dirt. They soon relax and revel in the feel of the soil between their fingers.

You are a gardener if you have any plant at all. The crucial point is that you care about growing something.

IT'S MY PLANT

A showy pot plant, with its opening buds and technicolour effect, standing in your child's bedroom will catch his eyes as soon as he opens them every morning. He may get even more satisfaction from 'his' plant if it is placed in a spot used by all the family. They are bound to admire it, making him feel really proud.

Plants that give easy results for little effort are ideal. Draw a feeding chart together and teach your child how to water the plant properly. Make it his responsibility so that he can truly say, 'It's my plant' – the fact that you may have to remind him to water and feed it occasionally can stay your secret!

Cyclamens – graceful beauties

Let your gardener pick the colour he wants and buy a plant with many closed buds on vigorous stems.

Correct watering is vital. Cyclamen corms and leaves dislike water on them, so watering should be done from below or just inside the rim of the pot. Teach your child to feel the soil before watering and never to add water to damp compost. Correct watering, a little care and a sunny window sill will ensure a colourful winter.

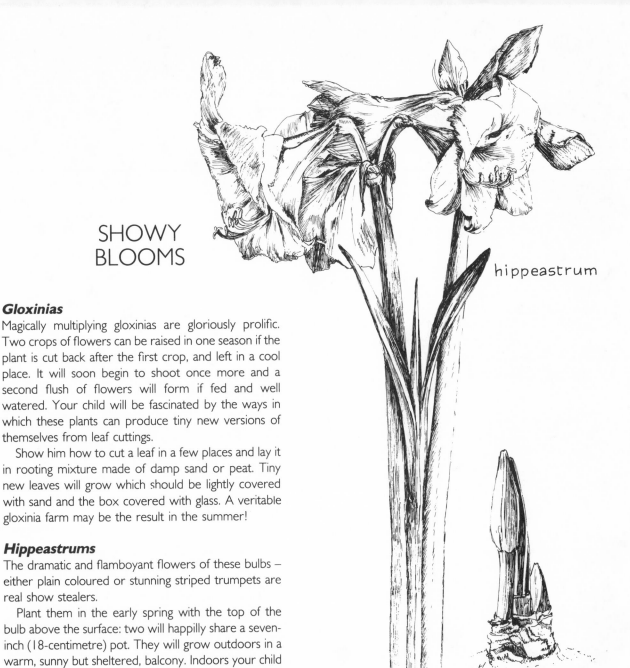

SHOWY BLOOMS

hippeastrum

Gloxinias

Magically multiplying gloxinias are gloriously prolific. Two crops of flowers can be raised in one season if the plant is cut back after the first crop, and left in a cool place. It will soon begin to shoot once more and a second flush of flowers will form if fed and well watered. Your child will be fascinated by the ways in which these plants can produce tiny new versions of themselves from leaf cuttings.

Show him how to cut a leaf in a few places and lay it in rooting mixture made of damp sand or peat. Tiny new leaves will grow which should be lightly covered with sand and the box covered with glass. A veritable gloxinia farm may be the result in the summer!

Hippeastrums

The dramatic and flamboyant flowers of these bulbs – either plain coloured or stunning striped trumpets are real show stealers.

Plant them in the early spring with the top of the bulb above the surface: two will happilly share a seven-inch (18-centimetre) pot. They will grow outdoors in a warm, sunny but sheltered, balcony. Indoors your child can measure the growth daily and admire the several flowers that open on one stem. After the flowers have died, continue watering until the leaves die down and store the bulbs for next year.

bulb and shoot

IT'S IN THE BAG

The marvellous Baccto Potting Soil can solve your child's gardening worries. It stays moist if he forgets to water it occasionally and the mixture is there ready for planting, sterilized to exclude pests and weeds.

If your child wants a garden of his own, why not try a Baccto bag of tomatoes? A sunny balcony or garden corner will be ideal.

Sturdy, bushy plants are best. New varieties need little or no staking and yield bunches of fruit. Place the bag in a sunny spot and cut some openings in it, one for each plant, and not too large so that the moisture is retained. Put a plant in each hole and firm it in well. Water regularly and give them a boost with tomato fertilizer when the trusses are forming.

Birds love tomatoes, so you may have to net them. Certain types of bushy tomatoes need not have the flowers limited to four trusses, a common practice with other tomatoes, but it certainly produces better quality fruit if production is limited slightly. Choose the stems that are to be allowed to develop full bunches and take off a few flowers on weaker ones. Watering should be stepped up as the plants get taller.

STRAWBERRY DELIGHT

Imagine relaxing on a hot summer's afternoon with a bowl of juicy strawberries and thick cream. Unless you live in the country and have a herd of Jersey cows it's difficult to produce your own cream, but you can grow your own plump, mouth-watering strawberries on the tiniest balcony.

Strawberries can be grown successfully in an earthenware pot, taking up minimal ground space. (Special pots are sold for this purpose, with pockets all around the sides.) The plants must have the sun, so 'portable' strawberries are an excellent idea as you can move the container to a sunnier spot if necessary. You can also turn the pot occasionally so that all sides get some sunshine. If no pot is available, I have seen strawberries grown in gutter piping; arranged pergola-fashion, they received sunshine and hung down enticingly.

Preparing the pot

These glorious berries will need a rich diet. Your child can ensure that all the plants receive this by inserting a perforated pipe into the centre of the pot when filling it with soil. This funnels water down to the lowest plants. Very refined gardening techniques can be added to the basics when strawberry growing. This pipe can be surrounded with fine mesh and the gap between the pipe and mesh filled with manure or other plant food. This way the plants get a rich feed when they drink.

Ensure good drainage with crocks and stones at the base, then fill the pot with a rich soil mixture, adding manure and bone meal or general fertilizer, up to the level of the first holes. Plant your first layer of plants and firm them down. It is a good idea not to plant all the layers at one time: let a few layers settle and plant the next row a few days later so that they do not sink

strawberries in special
earthenware pot

inwards. Protect from birds and keep an eye out for slugs. Keep up the watering throughout the growing season which begins in spring. The berries are ripe when they are that glorious red colour that makes you want to pick them from the pot and pop them into your mouth.

SMALL IS BEAUTIFUL

Miniature gardens are entrancing indoors or out and give scope for artistic designs and effects with water and rocks that may not be possible on a large scale. They have another valuable attribute – they can be cared for by an invalid. For someone who can't get about, even temporarily, the cultivation of a mini-landscape in a container or tray offers hours of rewarding entertainment.

Outdoor gardening is certainly easier, but indoor growing is just as rewarding. Bright sunshine is a pre-requisite and a careful watch for mildew and harmful insects will be essential.

Miniature roses will grow indoors, and a miniature cypress such as *Chamaecyparis pisifera* will add height and scale.

Water adds yet another dimension, and little containers can be sunk into the soil and edged with

alpine garden

COWBOY'S CACTUS GARDEN

Wild west heroes often ride across the desert. You can make your own desert landscape quite easily.

You will need an old tray or shallow container and adult help to drill some holes in the bottom, then cover it with pieces of broken flower pots. Put some gravel over this and then make a layer of soil or potting mixture. Plant some cacti and succulent plants in the soil and finish off with another layer of gravel for a true desert look. Add a few rocks. Some plants, such as lithops grow on stones and, look just like them, so plant some of them among the cacti. Remember to

rocks to give a natural effect. A tiny rush, *Acorus gramineus pusillus*, looks natural growing alongside the water. Little paths, bridges and rocks give the mini-gardener scope for design.

Good drainage is a must. Drill holes in troughs or old sinks and scatter a layer of broken terracotta pieces on the bottom. Cover this with a layer of peat and then a layer of potting mixture and you're ready. The sight of even a small surface ready to be worked on is as inviting to a mini-gardener as a blank canvas to a painter.

Insert some rocks *into* the soil: in real life rocks are seldom strewn loosely on the surface but are partly buried. In their natural home, high up in the mountains, alpines have developed a dwarf compact habit, perfectly formed in diminutive detail and ideal for mini-gardens. Miniature roses appeal, not just for their

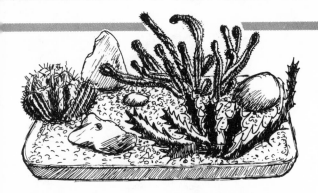

wear gardening gloves, as cacti are quite prickly. If you can't find a pair to fit, fold a piece of paper into a thick strip and use this as a collar around the plant. It will help you to grip it and will not damage the cactus.

Cacti need light, sunshine and good ventilation, but no water during the autumn and winter and only a little in spring and summer. Don't worry if they seem to shrivel a little in winter, they will flower much better if left without water during these months.

The great thing about your cactus garden is that it doesn't need much attention, and will survive long periods when you are away at another ranch.

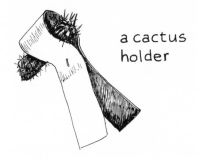

a cactus holder

beauty but for their charming names. *Rosa roulettii* is the tiniest rose; and who could resist Cinderella or Sweet Fairy. Some enthusiasts grow only roses in their miniature gardens, creating trellised arbours and tiny paths with minute ornaments and birdbaths, but for variety, children may want to mix flowers with trailing and mat covering plants, creating a world in which their minds can wander for hour after hour.

A DOLLS' HOUSE GARDEN

You too may become engrossed in creating a garden of the imagination, fashioning landscapes that echo the textures and colours of real life, modelling miniature features, substituting lentils for cobbles, tinted sawdust for grass, or the textured wallpaper which can simulate a rough surface.

Place the dolls' house on a rigid board and draw out features – driveway and patio and so on. Their scale must correspond to the scale of the house itself: trees should be the correct height in relation to windows.

Nature seldom produces a totally flat landscape – there are slopes and hollows. Children can make screwed-up lumps of newspaper to be clad in papiér mâché, and gauze bandages over a wire mesh frame can be covered in plaster. Make sure that details are carved into this before it dries; other material can also be stuck on. Make rock-like imprints from crumpled foil pressed onto wet plaster, then peel off later.

Nature's palette is subtle and varied. Remember that no tree is one green or bark one brown. Encourage a child to capture these tones with paint.

For foliage, dried heathers may be stripped and new leaves applied from bits of foam, dry lichen or a loofah. Scattered tea leaves resemble fallen leaves. Ponds or puddles may be created with glue over blue paint and foam produced with a squirt of snowspray left over from Christmas, or Epsom salts on wet paint.

Experiment together, finding tiny substitutes for reality.

BOTTLE GARDENS

In the section on plant transpiration (page 17) a plastic bag was put over the plant and the water condensed on the inside surface and ran down to the plant. This is the self-watering process that makes sealed bottle gardens (terraria) work so well. Unsealed ones need watering.

The Victorians made elaborate glass plant cases, but in our plastic age your child can make one simply by cutting up a plastic cold-drinks bottle and using the bottom part for his garden.

Alternatively, and much prettier if you have one, a large glass sweet jar, goldfish bowl or giant bulbous bottle make ideal 'mini-world' containers. Old rectangular fish-tanks can be used with a sheet of glass as a lid.

Pruning is best done with a razor blade inserted into the end of a soil firmer. Razor blades MUST be used carefully and it may be safer if parents do this.

soil firmer
(cork on knitting needle)
spoon attached
to pencil

BOTTLING UP

All bottle gardens need a little charcoal to keep the soil sweet, plus a layer of drainage material — gravel or small stones laid at the bottom of the jar. Make a funnel from stiff card to use when pouring this into the bottle. Pour a layer of sterilized potting soil on top of the gravel. The neck of the bottle will be too small to allow you to get your hand in to press down the soil, so poke a knitting needle into a cork and use this for pressing. A spoon attached to a long stick or pencil makes an ideal spade; and an old fork similarly wired to a stick will be the perfect tool for raking.

Down to planting

You will need tiny ferns and miniature foliage plants. The 'polka-dot' plant with its pretty pink and green leaves is ideal, and miniature ivies or baby's-tears make good ground covers. Maranta, the prayer plant, is interesting to watch with its peculiar leaves, and African violets will thrive in the steamy 'jungle' atmosphere. Miniature roses can be grown in bottles, but need to be sprayed in summer to protect them against aphids. Herbs, too, will take to this enclosed life: try thyme or parsley to start with.

Not too wet and not too dry...

Once your child has planted everything, get him to spray, squirt or syringe water into the bottle. (Water pistols have their uses after all!) Make sure he doesn't saturate the soil. You will need to keep a careful check at first to establish the moisture level. When the atmosphere in the bottle is perfect, there will be a slight film of moisture on the inside of the bottle and it can be closed up. If it is too wet, the plants will not flourish and too much vapour will cloud your view of the plants. If this happens, open the lid to allow a little evaporation. If the soil in the bottle has become sodden, you will notice beads of water forming on the margins of the leaves: open and allow evaporation to lower the moisture level. Most bottle garden plants prefer a light spot but avoid direct sunlight.

Flowering plants will need the lid removed regularly and wiped. This prevents too much moisture falling on the flowers. Ferns on the other hand prefer the lid left on at all times. By careful observation at first you should easily settle into carefree life with your bottle garden, once the correct moisture level is established.

It is essential to examine healthy young plants for insects before planting, as pests thrive in these bottles if they become established. This is why sterilized soil is a must.

Ferns and mosses will do well in weed-free peat.

As you lower your little plants gently into the bottle, hold them with a tool made from a wire coat-hanger. Bend the hanger straight and make a small spiral bend at one end. Slot the plant into this and lower it down. Use your knitting needle and cork tool to press the soil firmly around the plant. Chopsticks, toasting forks and knitting needles will all come in handy, and there's nothing better than an old, fine paintbrush to introduce insecticide or remove a bug.

MAKE A MOSS GARDEN

A moss garden is another ideal bottle subject: or a combination of mosses and ferns. Scavenge in walls and churchyards for soft, velvety moss. Some mosses are protected. Find out which they are – your local library should be able to help you – and be careful not to disturb them. The best places to find moss are damp, dank corners, but don't remove it all. Leave a fair amount behind so that it can reproduce and will not be wiped out by your picking it.

Once you have gathered the moss, put clean gravel at the bottom of your container – a fish tank is ideal – and then a layer of decaying plant matter covered with a layer of sterilized soil. Next arrange the mosses artistically adding some bark with lichen for more effect if you can find some. If you intend keeping the lid off, you will need to water and feed regularly, but condensation will do the job if the lid is to be kept on.

Remember that mosses are happiest if they are planted in a little of the soil in which you gathered them. Keep the bottle in a shady spot: you found the mosses in a dark, damp place so try to recreate those conditions.

BRIGHTEN UP YOUR WINDOWSILL

Delight passers-by and make the outlook soft and pleasing for those indoors with a window-box garden. Improve the view with a tiny landscape that you and your child can control, distracting the eye from any ugly features seen from the window.

Window-boxes are available in timber, treated for protection against weather. These, or troughs of cement, concrete, stone or terracotta, are attractive alternatives to the ubiquitous plastic.

Life is tough out there exposed to the wind, storms and pollution. Window-boxes tend to dry out quickly, so plant hardy choices and check that they are suited to the aspect. With young gardeners, a sunny spot will improve the plants' chances of survival.

There are several plants that are ideal for planting in window-boxes (see list page 125), but for staying power and attractive flowering all through summer, many enthusiasts swear by geraniums – there's a wide variety to choose from. Begonias and petunias are other safe choices and nasturtiums will trail attractively over the side.

Designed to please
Although the rectangular trough seems an unexciting shape, the plants chosen to fill it can create a well-balanced design. Taller plants are accents or focal points in the centre or back, colourful blooms fill in the centre, and droopy pendulous plants hang down and conceal the box. Offer your child a mixture and discuss the plants' habits. Some permanent plants may remain over the winter – ivies, junipers or little cypresses. These make up the basic skeleton of each year's design. Coloured foliage, silver or grey, bronze or yellow-gold, set off flowers and can be used as fillers or contrasting background. For some, this exercise is like painting and needs much care and thought.

PREPARING A WINDOW-BOX

First, find a suitable box and ask an adult to drill drainage holes in the bottom if there are none already there. While this is being done, you can put a couple of pieces of wood on the windowsill for the box to stand on: this improves drainage. Before you put the soil or compost in, line the bottom with broken pots, stones or gravel. Once it's filled with earth, the box will be too heavy for you to carry to the window yourself. Ask an adult to help you and also to ensure that the box is firmly fixed and will not work loose. Now you can begin planting – either sinking plants in pots into the soil or planting them straight into it. (The soil needs renewing annually.)

DON'T LEAN OUT TOO FAR WHILE GARDENING, you could end up having a nasty fall. It's much safer to use a spoon and a fork attached to long sticks with a little florist's wire. Someone may buy you small gardening forks and trowels with long handles. You'll also need a small, light watering can (water is quite heavy), and dibbers for planting. (Wooden spoon handles are just as good, and old kitchen spatulas are handy for patting and firming the earth around the plants.)

BALCONY GARDENS

Anyone lucky enough to have a balcony, patio, or flat roof, can turn it into a colourful garden oasis in a desert of concrete. On page 125 there's a list of just a few of the plants that are suitable for growing in these situations.

People with balcony gardens can be imaginative in their choice of containers; there are terracotta pots on sale; oil drums that are easily painted can usually be had for nothing; boxes, baskets, fibre-glass urns, barrels, tubs … this list is almost endless.

Because balconies are exposed to strong winds at times, climbing plants, such as roses and vines, should be secured to a trellis, and boxes and containers held firmly in place.

The ideal patio is sunny and protected where herbs, tomatoes, strawberries in a barrel, even an apple tree, as well as a profusion of flowering plants from fuchsias to lobelias can all be grown. But shady areas can be the home for climbers such as honeysuckle, clematis and ivies. Ferns will flourish in the shade and so will hydrangeas.

And there is one major advantage to container gardening. Purpose-made soil mixtures can be used to grow plants that require different soils. Roses can grow alongside rhododendrons.

The top layer of soil in containers should be covered with a mulch. This might be granite, gravel or bark chips, or decayed leaf material, all of which will be a barrier against the drying force of sun and wind.

PLANTING SPRING BULBS

The magical way that spring bulbs pop up out of the seemingly lifeless earth after their long sleep, awakens gardeners old and young to the delights of the new season.

Children find bulbs solid and much easier to handle than fragile seedlings, so they are ideal for tiny toddlers. Decide on a selection of early and late flowering bulbs, discuss and plan the layout with older children. List the bulbs, noting their height and colour and blooming season, so that a thoughtful designer can spend a little time thinking this out. Remember that bulbs usually look best in groups or clumps, rather than dotted in ones and twos.

With the plan agreed, planting can begin. Use the bulb chart to work out how deep the bulbs should go and how far apart they should be, and after planting one or two yourself, allow children of six or seven to take over in well prepared and raked soil.

Water lightly and forget about them for the severest part of the winter.

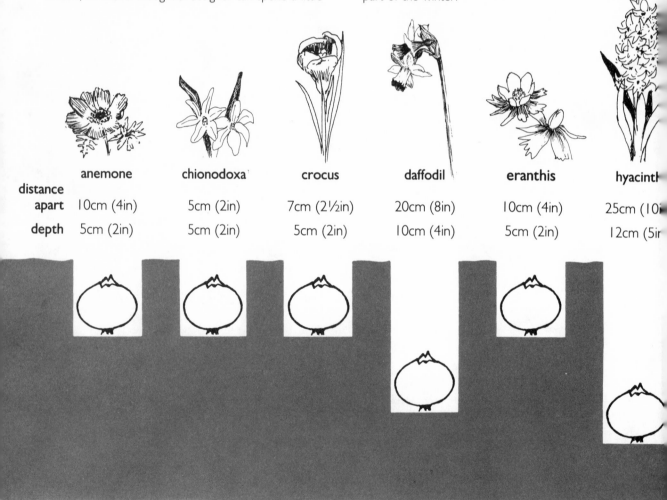

	anemone	chionodoxa	crocus	daffodil	eranthis	hyacinth
distance apart	10cm (4in)	5cm (2in)	7cm (2½in)	20cm (8in)	10cm (4in)	25cm (10
depth	5cm (2in)	5cm (2in)	5cm (2in)	10cm (4in)	5cm (2in)	12cm (5ir

As the ground begins to warm up and the hours of daylight increase, talk about this and keep a careful watch for the shoots emerging through even the hardest soil. Water when necessary: some spring days can be quite hot and there can be dry spells. One by one the shoots will swell and buds will form: your child should be thrilled as 'his' bulbs bloom day by day, and if he is sad when they fade, their fleeting beauty can be preserved by pressing the flowers. (See page 99).

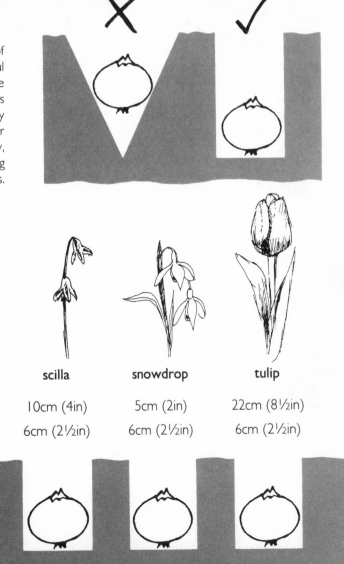

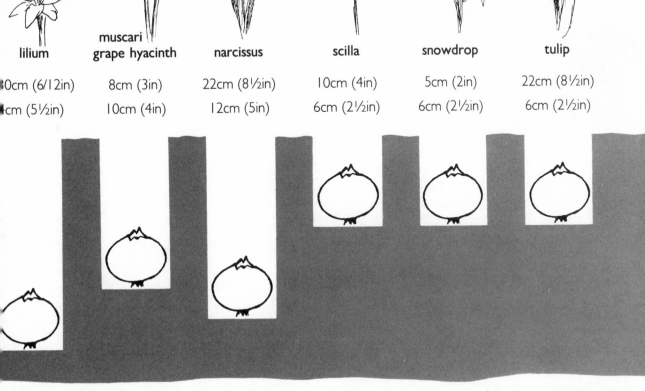

lilium	muscari grape hyacinth	narcissus	scilla	snowdrop	tulip
0cm (6/12in)	8cm (3in)	22cm (8½in)	10cm (4in)	5cm (2in)	22cm (8½in)
cm (5½in)	10cm (4in)	12cm (5in)	6cm (2½in)	6cm (2½in)	6cm (2½in)

ANNUAL TREATS

Transform a little patch by mid-summer into a riot of glorious colour. Choose hardy annuals (see the list on page 124). Show your young assistant how to prepare the soil by incorporating compost and digging over well, then raking it finely. Children love sifting the soil; it's such a fun job watching it rain down through the wire mesh and there are usually volunteers for this task.

As children become more experienced they will rise to the challenge of growing annuals from seed: gently pricking out and handling the seedlings is a skill that comes with practice. Many young children lack the dexterity required to plant the delicate new roots firmly in the fine soil. For them established seedlings will be more successful. You will have to demonstrate how to prise them gently apart and check that the holes are the right depth. Enlarge or mark these holes with a dibber or the handle of a wooden spoon. The soil must be firmly pressed around the base of the little plant with no air pockets in which roots could dry out. On the other hand, don't let your child squeeze little plants to death.

The seedlings, having survived the rigours of planting, will appreciate a light sprinkle from the watering can.

Water and warmth

If you have a spare plantlet or two, show your child what happens to the plant in a torrential downpour, then he will understand why the fine rose is necessary on the watering can or hosepipe. In very hot climates little seedling hats are available to shield tiny seedlings from the hot sun for the first couple of weeks.

If the weather is exceptionally hot just after planting, you can make your own by folding stiff plastic sheets into cones, stapling them on to sticks (popsicle sticks are ideal) so that they can be firmly poked into the ground. Set them at an angle, like beach umbrellas, and make certain they don't prevent water getting to the seedlings.

If spring is hot and dry, make certain that the little plants do not dry out. If, as is more usual, spring is wet, keep a close watch for mildew. Remove any affected plants to avoid it spreading. Annuals are not described as 'hardy' for nothing: they will survive a great deal and will give your child enormous pleasure.

Cultivating

Let your little gardener gently fork around the plants when necessary to keep down weeds and aerate the soil. He can watch out for slugs and snails and other threats to his crop.

(See page 122 for suggestions for dealing with insect pests without using dangerous chemicals.)

Picking

Once the glory of the longed-for blooms is achieved, dead-heading and picking will prolong their flowering period. Pansies, sweetpeas and roses benefit from picking and are a joy to have in the house.

Self-seeding

Many of the hardy annuals are self-seeding, so, towards the end of summer leave a few to seed themselves. By next spring the new seedlings will be naturalized and tougher still to survive the rigours of life at the hands of inexperienced but enthusiastic gardeners.

Gardening gadgets

Technology is being applied to gardening just as it is to every aspect of our lives today. Pelleted seed is a modern development, and many are available in little starter kits, coming complete with the planting medium, little propagator and seeds. This type of seed buying is naturally more costly, but will save hunting around for a suitable box, potting compost and transparent lid. Children can watch the seeds start to shoot indoors.

Polystyrene seed boxes, neatly sectioned to give each plant its own little square, come with a 'pusher' grid that gently eases out the plants when you are ready to transplant them. Simply push the grid into the box from beneath, and each seedling emerges with its own cube of soil. These gadgets may seem gimmicky to an experienced gardener, but when working with children they may make all the difference between success or failure.

A REAL GROWTH INDUSTRY

Interest in gardening has mushroomed in the past few years, and shelf after shelf of books on the subject have been written. The aim of this book is to try to encourage appreciation of the whole world of nature, and therefore I have not put in much about 'gardening' techniques and dos and don'ts. Use all the information at your disposal – your local library, gardening centre, gardening club (if there's one nearby), radio programmes and so on. Above all, never be afraid to ask advice from experienced gardeners: they like nothing better than passing on the information that years of experience have taught them. May your fingers, too, turn green!

SUNNY GIANTS

A giant sunflower grows like Jack's beanstalk, with its sunny head seemingly smiling. They grow at an amazing rate and the seedhead is easily dried after the flower has wilted. Notice how the seeds are arranged in a pattern, and keep them for seed collage (page 104).

GROWING YOUR OWN VEGETABLES

An easy and quick crop of radishes makes a good start to vegetable gardening. Ancient Egyptians enjoyed these sparkling red roots, so they have been around for some time!

Prepare the soil carefully. It must be brought to a fine tilth – all the lumps broken down and the texture fine. Incorporate plenty of humus or peat and decayed manure. Sow seeds thinly by making a sharp fold in a piece of paper and placing the seeds in it. Tap the paper and the seeds will be sprinkled out. Lightly rake the seed into the upper 2·5 centimetres (1 inch) of soil. In dry spells keep the bed moist. Within a month pull up the radishes and enjoy the tangy taste.

Carrots can be grown alongside radishes, for the latter will be lifted well before the carrots mature. Sow the seeds finely and thin out to 10 centimetres (4 inches). Water during dry weather.

You can also grow herbs as a border around your vegetable garden; they help to keep certain pests away (see page 123).

This outdoor vegetable gardening is best done in summer and in a sunny open spot.

GROWING POTATOES INDOORS

Potatoes, though usually grown in trenched ground in the open, will grow indoors in plastic bags! All you have to do is prepare two heavy duty bags. In one, puncture a few holes and place inside the second. Put some compost in the one with the holes. When the tubers have short sprouts, rub off all but the two strongest. Put them into the compost and put the bags into a warm place, an airing cupboard or somewhere warm in the kitchen. After about three months you will have a delicious meal of new potatoes.

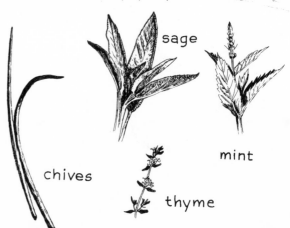

sage

mint

chives

thyme

DIARY, DIARY, HOW DID MY GARDEN GROW?

Creative gardeners keep regular diaries from year to year. You and your children might like to do the same. There's no need to write elaborate notes: keep entries short and simple, and illustrate the pages with photographs and diagrams. Many children love to draw, and older ones often become interested in taking snaps, acquiring both the skill and the patience to photograph the plants grown in the garden and the insect and animal visitors.

Note successful planting schemes and good colour combinations. Comment on unfortunate failures.

Record the seasonal changes visible from a window, and which plants flower together.

Make a list of the plants grown. How long did the seeds take to germinate? When did they achieve full bloom? How long did they last?

Press some leaves and petals between the pages. Make a spore print (see page 91), a rubbing (page 103) and in the months of winter when the garden outside is grey and bleak you can look back on how beautiful it was in spring, summer and autumn and plan how you can bring it back to glorious colour again.

MAY

flowers

trees

vegetables

birds

insects

animals

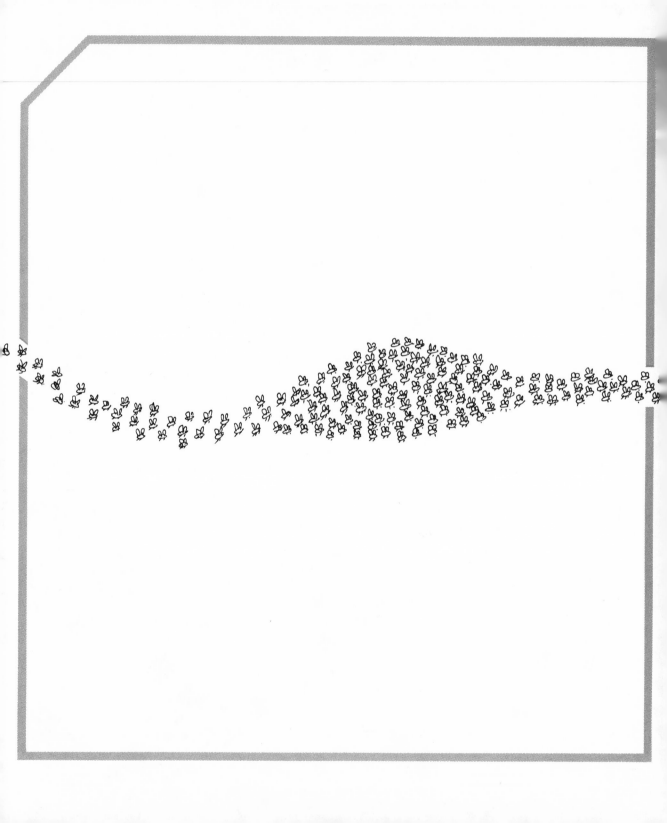

GARDEN VISITORS

The restless cuckoo absent long,
And twittering swallows' chimney song,
With hedgerow crickets notes that run
From every bank that fronts the sun.
And swarthy bees about the grass
That stop with every bloom they pass:
And every minute, every hour,
Keep teasing weeds that wear a flower
And toil, and children's humming joys
For there is music in the noise.

John Clare

BUTTERFLIES

Rippling, crunching caterpillars seem to bear no resemblance to the delicate fragile butterflies they become, and this transformation is miraculous each time you see it.

Observing the four stages from egg to imago is unforgettable and need not involve breeding them yourself. Finding caterpillars of the Privet Hawk is easy in privet hedges during July and August when they are about three inches long, and a clump of nettles will be host to many caterpillar species. Many of them pupate in the soil and the adults emerge the following summer. The Red Admiral, Common Blue and the Small Copper are found all over the country and there are few children who do not know the Cabbage Whites, so noticeable with their white silken wings fluttering against the garden greenery.

Holly Blues are happy in town or country and obligingly produce two generations each year. It is possible to spot the caterpillars in spring, feeding on holly blossoms, and then the autumn generation on the ivy.

Butterflies may be passing through a garden from a nearby wild patch, or they may be migrating long distances and alight in your garden as a restorative refuge. To offer welcome food to these winged visitors, plant some nectar bearing plants (See page 56) and add thistle, dock and nettles in wild corners of the garden for caterpillars.

Butterflies will feed on the juices of rotting fruit and children will be delighted to see their hollow, tubular tongues uncurl and suck up the juice, then fold neatly away again. The word 'proboscis' is a bit of a tongue twister for some, but you will doubtless be asked if you can spell it by some child who has come across it at school.

Interested youngsters will enjoy a trip to one of the butterfly farms dotted around the country. Those lucky enough to live in Cincinnati can visit its zoo which houses a Butterfly Aviary, where you can admire the beauty of many species of these winged wonders.

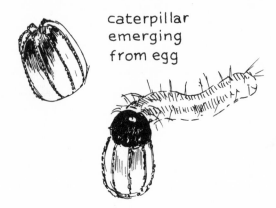

caterpillar emerging from egg

COMPLETE CHANGE

To help your child observe the butterfly life cycle more closely, caterpillars can be kept in a simple cage (see page 54). At times the fat greedy caterpillar will stop feeding and moult, attaching itself with silken threads to a leaf or twig. The old skin will split and the caterpillar resumes gorging as the new skin hardens. When finally filling the new skin almost to bursting point, it is ready to pupate.

The caterpillar will stop feeding and change colour: some will spin silky pads to attach themselves to leaves

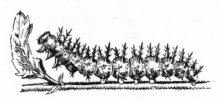

caterpillar

or twigs, others pupate in the soil. When it is suspended from a twig by the last pair of legs, you may see the creature split its skin yet again with one great acrobatic wriggle, freeing itself of the last skin. It may become difficult to spot the pupae as they are well camouflaged, their only form of defence – they need it.

Great fun to observe are the species that spin a cocoon before the final moult; the fine silken threads are clearly visible as the caterpillar spins a protective casing around its body. In this it will spend the next stage of its life during which the insect's body is completely changed.

The life cycle of different species varies a great deal, so it pays to find out how long it will be before the butterfly emerges from the pupa, which species are most common in your neighbourhood and what food they will need when they emerge.

To store the pupa, remove all remnants of plant material from it as these can cause mould to form. The pupa should be stored where it won't dry out, ideally in an airtight box or a tin in the fridge.

About three weeks before it is due to emerge, bring it in to a warmer place, and remember that when the butterfly finally emerges it will want to climb towards the light to dry out its wings. Put the almost mature pupa into a wooden cage with netting at the top, and containing some twigs. The fragile butterfly will cling to the twigs as it dries its wings. Feed it and provide water for three days and then release it into the garden. Watch as it flutters around from plant to plant enjoying freedom.

Butterfly breeding can be a rewarding hobby. Should you wish to find out more about it there are butterfly societies you can join.

Most children are captivated by butterflies and love to draw and paint them. They may also like to make a butterfly collage with scraps of paper or cloth: it will keep them engrossed for hour after hour.

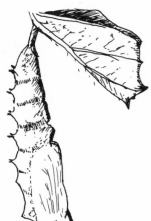

pupa of butterfly

butterfly emerging

butterfly

MAKE A CATERPILLAR CAGE

If you would like to watch a caterpillar munching and moulting at close quarters, make a simple cage – it's very easy.

All you need is a coffee jar or biscuit tin, some rigid plastic sheeting, a small flowerpot, a plant cutting and some garden soil.

Puncture a few holes in the lid of the jar or tin for ventilation and put it to one side for the moment.

Take a cutting of the plant on which the caterpillar was found or plant a small root of it in your flowerpot. Fill the base of the container with soil, and sink the flowerpot in it. Next, fit the plastic sheet inside the rim of the container to form a cylinder and fix the lid to the top to hold it firmly in the circular shape. You have made a caterpillar cage!

You can make it even more simply if you decide to use fresh stems cut daily, rather than pot up a cutting or root. Put a little vase of water in the soil instead of the flowerpot. Cover it with paper or Plasticine, leaving a hole for the plant stem. The cover is a safeguard for the caterpillar, as without it the animal could fall into the water and drown.

When they are ready to pupate, some caterpillars will need a couple of twigs placed into the soil from which to hang. Others will burrow into the soil until they are ready to shed the pupal skin and emerge as the imago or adult butterfly.

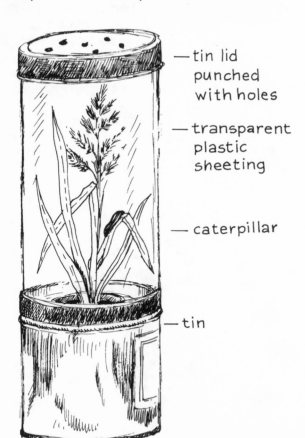

— tin lid punched with holes

— transparent plastic sheeting

— caterpillar

— tin

A CAGE FOR THE BUTTERFLY

The time it takes for the adults to emerge varies from species to species. Check how long it will take for your species to mature and use the time when there is nothing to see to make a large cage for the butterflies.

A large wooden cage with netting on top will suit them. Place twigs inside it so that they can climb up on these. A day or two before you think the pupae are ready, put them carefully in the new cage and spray the cage, pupae and all to keep it moist. A fine mist from a spray gun or water pistol will do for this job.

First, a drink ...
The first need of the newly emerged butterfly will be water, so spray in such a way that droplets form on the netting and twigs so that they can drink.

moths

THERE'S A TIGER IN THE GARDEN

The most evocative names are given to moths: Humming-bird Hawk Moth, Death's Head Hawk Moth, Goat Moth, Hop Moth, Elephant Hawk and Garden Tiger are a few that belie the size of the bearer of the name.

Moths are more than fluttering idiots attempting sizzling suicide on light bulbs. There are 2,000 species of them with widely varying habits which make them a fascinating subject for study.

'What's the difference between moths and butterflies?' is a question every parent will be asked. Generally, moths are night creatures and butterflies active by day: but the creatures confound the issue as several moths are about by day.

Study the wings with your child and notice how moths fold their wings along the sides of the body to form a triangular or delta shape: butterflies close theirs upright along the back. Butterflies' wings have separate front and rear sections, the moths are able to hook these sections together.

Moths have coarse, feathery antennae, butterflies have finer, threadlike ones with little lumps on the end.

Compare the graceful narrow body of the butterfly with the fatter moths which seem like ugly sisters compared to the Cinderella butterflies, for all their fine colours and clever camouflage designs.

... then something to eat

On pages 56 and 57 there is a list of nectar-bearing plants. Find out which is your species' favourite plant and put a few flowers into the cage for your butterfly to feed upon. You might like to offer these delicate creatures a weak solution of honey, sugar and salt if there are no plants available.

Mix together ½ teaspoon of honey, a ½ teaspoon of sugar and ¼ teaspoon of salt in a cup of water. Soak a piece of cottonwool in this and leave it in a saucer in the cage.

SWOOPING AND LOOPING

Release them after a day or two and watch the butterflies. Try to determine the regular flight patterns of the different species you can see.

Look for low swoops in a straight line, or low, looping zig-zag patterns: others will adopt a steady fluttering in a straight line.

NIGHT FLIGHTS

To watch nocturnal moths, cover a flashlight with red tissue so they will not be disoriented by the light and take it into the garden. The moths will be hovering round nectar-bearing flowers that have developed night scents to attract them, and colours which can be seen by insects in the twilight. You can attract moths to the bark of a tree by painting it with a sugar syrup.

BUTTERFLY GARDENING

Attract butterflies to your garden with old-fashioned country garden perennials, nectar-bearing shrubs and flowers. Seek out roots from friends and divide clumps. Not only will your garden be colourful and much admired but you will all be delighted by the numbers of butterflies that visit your garden.

You may be lucky enough to watch the courtship behaviour of the insects you attract. Sight and scent both play an important part in this. In the butterflies the males give out a scent which attracts the female, among the moths it is usually the female who does so. Many male moths have extraordinarily sensitive smelling organs on their antennae and can smell a female's scent more than a mile away!

Try and find a freshly emerged Emperor female and put it in a muslin cage on a sunny afternoon. She will soon be surrounded by dozens of males, who may well stay in the garden to enjoy the plants that you have grown for them.

You can have lovely lilacs, buddleias and delicate bluebells, cheeky Michaelmas daisies and subtle heathers. Put in some polyanthus and petunias, and don't forget some herbs: not only will they attract the butterflies, they have more traditional uses, too. Caterpillars will feed on thistle, dock and nettles in an overgrown corner.

Many nectar-bearing plants will occur naturally: daisies and dandelions, for example. Unless you are aiming for the sort of manicured, smooth and closely cut lawn seen in adverts for lawnmowers, leave a corner of the garden wild where they can thrive.

To attract butterflies and bees, old-fashioned country-garden perennials, nectar-bearing shrubs and flowers are what you need. This list is by no means complete, but most of the plants in it are easy to get.

Ageratum

Alyssum (white)

Arabis (pink and white)

Aubretia

Birdsfoot trefoil

Bluebell

Buddleia (butterfly bush)

Campion

Candytuft

Catnip

Clover

Comfrey

Cowslip

Daisy

bluebe

cowslip

daisy

c

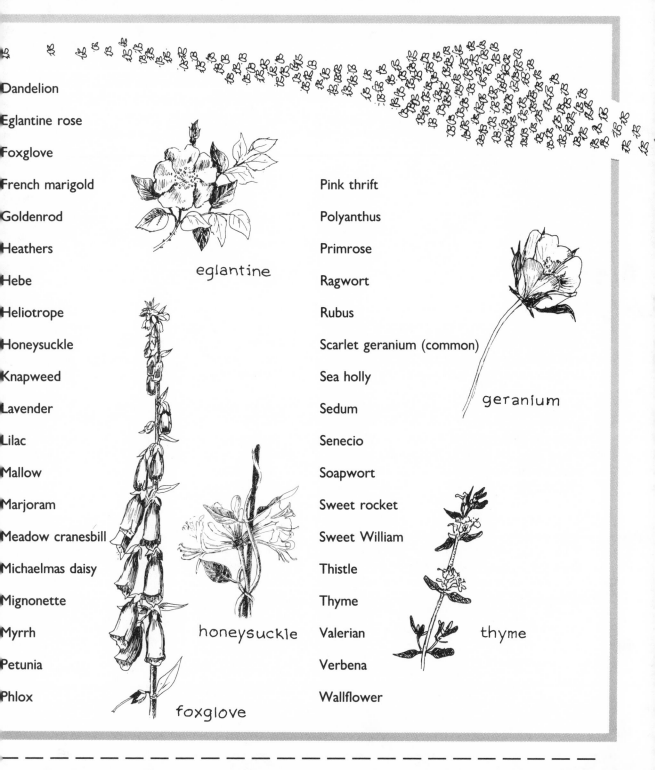

Dandelion

Eglantine rose

Foxglove

French marigold

Goldenrod

Heathers

Hebe

Heliotrope

Honeysuckle

Knapweed

Lavender

Lilac

Mallow

Marjoram

Meadow cranesbill

Michaelmas daisy

Mignonette

Myrrh

Petunia

Phlox

eglantine

Pink thrift

Polyanthus

Primrose

Ragwort

Rubus

Scarlet geranium (common)

Sea holly

Sedum

Senecio

Soapwort

Sweet rocket

Sweet William

Thistle

Thyme

Valerian

Verbena

Wallflower

geranium

honeysuckle

thyme

foxglove

HONEY BEES

The fascinating story of life in a beehive is told to children in most primary schools. Children are enthralled when they hear about a colony ruled by a Queen, with busy workers buzzing around and idle drones who are expelled in the autumn and die. Most youngsters are quick to become 'bee conscious', especially if they are encouraged to look at honey in a comb and at bees in garden or park. They will watch them diving into flowers in search of nectar, so talk about the bees' pollinating progress as they move from flower to flower.

Bees will enjoy all the nectar-bearing plants listed on pages 56 and 57, but are particularly fond of balm. According to John Parkinson, a great Elizabethan gardener, balm rubbed on the inside of the hive attracted bees because 'it draweth by the smell thereof to resort hither'. If you do succeed in attracting bees to your garden, they will particularly enjoy thyme, catnip, salvia, mint and blue-flowered borage, mignonette and hyssop which gives a flavour to the honey.

'How do they make the buzz?', 'How do they know their way back to the hive?' and 'How do they sting?' are just a few of the questions bee watching provokes.

The humming is made by the movement of the bees' wings as they fly, not by a voice box or, as some children imagine, the bees' engine. As the wings vibrate, the air around them also vibrates producing the buzzing noise that we can hear.

These attractive insects will roam up to 5 kilometres (3 miles) in search of food, and are skilled navigators within this radius, using the sun as a guide. They send out scouts, which, having located the source of food, return to tell the others about it through a unique form of dance, which expresses the type of food, its location and its distance from the hive. The scouts return to the find with other bees, and naturalists have observed their dances and marked the scouts to check this.

If a hive is moved to a spot within the feeding radius, the bees will return to the original spot, but will not be able to locate the new position of the hive because their sensors are confused by its proximity to the former location. To successfully move a hive a short distance you must first move it far away, thus 'reprogramming' the bees, and then back to a spot near the initial location.

Bees sting only in desperation to protect the hive. Their sting is the only weapon they have, sending poison through the fine, barbed tube. But when it is embedded in the victim, the bee cannot remove it, and when it flies off, the sting is ripped from the bee which dies a few minutes later.

Karl von Frisch, an Austrian biologist, studied bee behaviour and showed that the bees can distinguish colours. A bee given honey on a sheet of glass over a particular colour will return to that colour with co-workers even when the honey is wiped off and the surrounding colours changed or mixed. Only bright red seemed to confuse them.

WATCH IT FEED

If you would like to study a bee at close quarters, attract it with a stick, coated with honey. When it has settled, notice how the proboscis is rather different from that of the butterfly. The bee's is jointed and the insect uses it like a spoon: the butterfly uses its proboscis as if it were a drinking straw.

Do be careful, though. If the bee feels threatened it will sting in the last resort.

INDUSTRIOUS ANTS

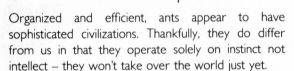

Organized and efficient, ants appear to have sophisticated civilizations. Thankfully, they do differ from us in that they operate solely on instinct not intellect – they won't take over the world just yet.

They are infinitely absorbing as they work, defend and labour with heavy burdens. The cumbersome loads they haul back to their nests are not simply food: sometimes they are the cocoons of other ant nests they have raided in order to rear slaves for their own ant colony.

There are more than 3,000 types of ants, all of which are pretty industrious. They range from red biting ants, to acrobatic ants that raise their abdomens to stand upside down if threatened. There are armies of little brown ants marching along pavements, and squads of flesh-eating ants munching their way across Africa. Ants stowed away on ships, travelled to distant places and set up colonies there.

Some ants, the Harvesters, collect and store food seeds, while others rear and protect aphids which they milk for their sticky honeydew. These ants carry the aphids out to pasture on our garden plants and 'milk' them by strok-ing their bodies, gobb-ling up the secreted substance as quick-ly as the aphids produce it.

Many ants have poor sight, relying on scent, touch and sound as well as vibration. They send out scouts to look for food. Flesh-eaters appear to plan attacks with the precision of military tacticians, sometimes encircling the prey with two flanks.

They build great ant cities and maintain a rigid class structure of slaves, workers and soldiers with a Queen who does nothing but lay eggs after her one moment of

flight during which she mates with a winged male. The males die shortly after the nuptial flight and the Queen returns to the ground, sheds her gossamer wings and starts her own colony.

The eggs that she lays grow into workers or soldiers: a few winged ants are reared, small males and larger

ANT-ICS

Look out for ant nests in earth, in roots of ferns and in rotted logs.

Can you spot ants raiding the nests of others, scurrying off with their booty – the white cocoons?

On a warm autumn evening, perhaps after a shower, watch for the flight of the winged ants on their one and only flight.

SEE HOW THEY RUN

Keep a close look out for a column of ants on the move and try and work out how they know where they are going.

Some types of ants navigate by scent trails laid by their colleagues. If the scent is obliterated, they cannot follow the trail. Wood ants navigate by the sun. If the trail is wiped out they keep on coming, constantly in the same direction. If they are moved to another spot they soon set off again facing the same way. Spray some cheap scent on a trail or put a large object in the path of the ant army and see what happens.

females. These are kept underground, fed and nurtured for their mating flights when the weather and season are deemed right – usually in autumn.

If it seems like the stuff of fiction to you, imagine how it must seem to your child, sitting there enthralled by the busy creatures, visualizing a scenario in which the ants do take over the world.

Auguste Forel, the great 'historian of the ants' became fascinated by the ant life he saw in his garden as a boy. Devoting the rest of his life to their study, he produced a heavy, definitive volume on these insects. Parents of children similarly fascinated may need reserves of patience when all other tasks lie neglected in favour of ant armies.

INSECTS ALL AROUND

Your garden is the playground of a host of other insects. There will be little ladybirds, long a favourite with children, doing a marvellous job on the greenfly: rosechafers eating in the roses, their metallic wings glistening in the sunlight. Carabids may be spotted looking for their lunch – snails, grasshoppers and other insects. Some enthusiastic children like to keep them as 'pets'. Feeding them is a gruesome task – carnivorous, they like the food they're used to!

My own children once kept a praying mantis as a free-roaming house pet. The fascination this produced was worth the rather startled expressions of some adults as they spotted it, sitting motionless with its praying front legs, ready to pounce on an unfortunate spider that crossed its path.

Noises in the grass

On warm summer evenings listen to the crickets chirping. As soon as you approach they infuriatingly stop, only to begin again as soon as you move away. It is the males which chirp, and together with the chorus of birds they make up nature's evensong. Crickets sing by rubbing the base of their wings together.

Grasshoppers, too, make a scratchy sound until they spring away through the grass at your approach. The male grasshopper has a row of tiny teeth on his inside back leg, visible only under magnification. As his legs move up and down, these teeth strike against the rigid veins in the wing, setting up the vibrations that we can hear. So can the females, for whom this lovesong is produced.

SNAILS

Many members of the mollusc family are sea dwellers, but earth dwelling snails have various adaptations to enable them to live on land. They are easily found after rain, or in damp shady spots on walls, overturned flowerpots or rocks. Have children hunt for snails (your plants will feel the benefit!) and have a look at the nostril-like opening at the back of the head through which they breathe. The snail's rasp-like tongue can be seen as it munches and shreds the plant material. The smaller pair of tentacles enable them to smell food, and there are simple eyes on the larger pair. Watch the tentacles withdraw if touched, then gradually reappear.

The snail will turn from side to side while moving forward, feeling with these sensitive tentacles. If threatened, the animal will withdraw entirely into the shell.

FOLLOW THE TRAIL

The trails left by these gastropods can be seen clearly early in the morning. In spite of stories about their slow pace, determined snails will climb the sides of a bucket or wall in a pretty impressive way, rippling along on a bed of slime.

Dust a snail trail with talcum powder to make it easier to follow.

Snails frequently return to the same spot to roost. See if the snails in your garden do this, by looking around for the hideout where they cluster and mark their shells with Liquid Paper or nail polish – a tiny dot is sufficient – so that you can identify them and see if they return to this spot regularly.

LETTING IT RIPPLE

To get a clear view of the rippling muscle contractions which propel the snail forwards, place one on a sheet of glass or inside a jam jar. Study the underside through the glass and see the ripples push the snail forward from the tail end.

TEST YOUR SNAIL'S SIGHT

Snails can see and feel their way through an obstacle course. Put a heap of snails in the centre of a circle of thick plastic. Around the circle place bricks and other barriers at intervals, leaving small gaps between them. The next morning, follow the trails and you will find that the snails have moved out through the gaps between the obstacles.

UP AND OVER

Mucous made by glands near the head forms a slimy cushion which hardens to form the tell-tale trails. Snails are able to move over sharp surfaces without damaging their feet. Their delicate sense of touch enables them to place the foot with exactly the correct pressure so that they can glide over rough stones on their gelatinous cushion. Place a few snails on rough surfaces and watch how skilfully they navigate when they come out of their shells and set off.

HEDGEHOGS

They succumb to traffic and fire in alarming numbers. Hiding under leaves makes them vulnerable to winter bonfires, so please look carefully before setting fire to a pile. Their response to all threats is to roll up into a prickly ball, and although this has protected them from their natural enemies, unfortunately it does not frighten away road traffic.

Leave one corner of the garden wild, providing some cover for little animals, and a hedgehog, grateful for a shady resting place, may shelter here. They rest under piles of branches or leaves in the daytime coming out at dusk to snuffle round the garden looking for worms, insects, grubs and snails. Although these little mammals are mainly insectivores, they are curious and adventurous with foods, tasting a wide variety of morsels.

A PRICKLY PAIR

In spring, courting hedgehog couples snort and circle one another for hours, the problem of approaching a mate covered with defensive spikes causing considerable delays!

Always interpreted as endearing little creatures hedgehogs intrigue children. Illustrators have shown hedgehogs with fruit impaled on their spines in order to carry it home, but observers say this is fanciful, and insist that no food is ever taken to the nest.

MAKE A HEDGEHOG SHELTER

Prop a plank of wood against a wall and secure it by putting a large stone or rock at the bottom to prevent it sliding down the wall. Leave a small gap between the plank and the wall and you may find a hedgehog taking shelter, especially if you camouflage it well.

Hedgehogs are said to like hollow pipes. Embed some in a sheltered corner of your garden or near a pond. They also like piles of logs as temporary cover.

You may see your little friend at night if you keep a careful watch and put out a tempting delicacy for it: a ripe apple may tempt the animal into the middle of the lawn.

MAKE A TASTY SNACK

A saucer of bread and milk, diluted with one part water to two parts milk, may well tempt a hedgehog, but set the saucer into the ground so that it is not easily tipped over. They have also been known to enjoy pet-food, bacon rind and food scraps, but as their insect-eating habits are such a help to gardeners, destroying many a garden pest, perhaps it is best that their diets should not be interfered with.

HARDWORKING WORMS

When digging the garden with your little helper, don't be surprised if he pauses very often and stares at the soil, fascinated by wriggling worms. These writhing creatures can be watched at leisure by making a wormery, and their contribution to gardening – aerating the soil with their tunnelling and feeding patterns – can be clearly seen.

First, watch the way worms move by contracting parts of their bodies: children often try this out on the floor for themselves. The worm will fix itself to the walls of its burrow with strong, hair-like setae protruding from its body. These can exert quite a force, and the worm may well need them to resist being yanked out of the hole by a bird.

Although they are equipped with female and male parts – they are hermaphrodite – worms still mate in pairs, rather than fertilize themselves, and you may see two worms doing this, lying side by side in a burrow.

Your child is bound to ask how they can dig without spades. They eat the soil as they burrow and pass it out of their bodies. And if he asks how many worms there are, tell him that in an average meadow, if all the worms were assembled and weighed, they would weigh more than all the livestock grazing in it.

FLASHLIGHT STUDY

Take a flashlight into the garden at night; tip-toe across the lawn where the earthworms will be looking for decaying leaves to pull into their burrows. Notice how they leave the tips of their bodies in their holes, then stamp your feet and watch them silently slip back in a flash.

WORMING THROUGH THE WORMERY

To make a wormery collect different sorts of soils from a few gardens to form layers of various textures and colours. Pack these into a glass jar, one layer on top of another to look like a multi-coloured cassata ice cream, and don't mix them together. If your container is too large, it will be some time before you will see the worms near the glass. Place a few decaying leaves on the top and then fetch the worms. They require moisture and must not be left to dry out on the surface where they will die if they cannot immediately burrow again. The best time to catch them is after a shower when they come to the surface. (In very hot, dry conditions they burrow deep into the earth, and may roll up and rest until the rains come.) Cover the side of your wormery with black paper or fabric to create the dark conditions that the worms enjoy and the industrious creatures will set to work tunnelling and mixing the layers of the soil. If you make the top layer a light sandy soil, you will easily see it mix with lower layers. They will draw the leaves into their burrow to feed and some will eat the soil itself, absorbing the organic matter with it. They will stay active as long as the wormery is moist and dark.

LIFE AFTER DARK

At night, the garden is alive with nocturnal creatures coming out to feed. A closer look at them will be interesting for your child and revealing to you. Now you know who's been eating the roses!

WATCHING WOODLICE

Woodlice are not really lice at all. They are not insects either, but members of the shrimp and crab family, the crustaceans. That makes them seem more acceptable right away to most parents! They are not harmful to the garden either, feeding as they do on decaying plant material.

Hiding in moist places they spend the day squeezed into crevices or beneath rocks or flowerpots. At night they come out safely in the dark. Let your child lift up a stone or flowerpot and gather a few as they scuttle for cover. Put them in a box lined with damp soil or wet blotting paper and cover it with a sheet of glass or plastic. Through this lid you can watch the woodlice huddle together, comfort in a crowd, as they hunt for cracks and angles in which to wedge themselves.

They take two years to reach their maximum size, moulting as they grow out of their skins. Always keep woodlice in a cool, shady place.

curled up woodlouse

A CLOSER WATCH

Woodlice are programmed for survival and will instinctively move towards damp spots. You can watch this in a controlled experiment. Put damp blotting paper in one corner of your box, leaving the rest bare. Add woodlice and watch how quickly they will go to the damp corner. Now shade one half of your box and shine bright light over the other half: the woodlice will make for the shade at once. If the area in brighter light is damp, while that in the shade is dry, they will choose shade, even abandoning a moist spot to do so.

Set a trap ...
Dig a little hole in the soil and lower an empty yoghurt carton in it. Bait it with an apple core and put a piece of slate or another flat object above the carton, raised up on a few stones. This allows the creatures to crawl along and fall in, but shelters them from the hot, morning sun and hides them from possible predators. Come back in the morning and see who has toppled into your trap. Chances are there will be earwigs and centipedes munching at the apple. Watch them and then put them back in the soil.

... to catch a millipede
Punch some holes in the sides of an empty tin and fill it with carrot or potato peelings. Fix a handle to it and bury it upright in the ground. After a few days pull the tin up by the handle and you're sure to find one or two of these multi-legged creatures in your trap.

Keep a check book
Check the traps at various times of the day to find out when the insects arrive. Place traps in different areas – in the lawn, under the hedge, in a compost heap – and note the assortment you catch. Record and compare the insect life in your traps. Was there more in one area? Did the weather play a part? You'll learn a lot about the habits and habitats of the insects in your garden.

WHO'S EATING WHO IN THE APPLE TREE?

Finding out who's eating who in the apple tree is an ongoing project, but it is not necessarily time-consuming. Observations can be easily squeezed into odd moments, even on a busy day and children may wish to keep a record of what is going on. Leaves need examining and bark, where it has come loose, may be sheltering various forms of life.

Fallen leaves and apples are especially interesting. Throughout the year there is an endless cycle of life being played out here, with ever more creatures being born, living out their allotted span, or being gobbled up, and the gobblers themselves being the diet of other, larger animals.

Now little caterpillars make a meal of the leaves and buds. They spin silken threads which keep leaves furled and twisted. Using this thread as an escape hatch, they lie within the leaf munching away and when a bird pokes its beak into it in search of a juicy morsel, the caterpillar lets itself down from the other end on his silk lifeline, waits until the coast is clear and then climbs back up into the leaf. Unfortunately, it's not fool- (or bird-) proof. The birds catch thousands of caterpillars before they can get away. Over a few weeks a nestful of baby birds can put away a few thousand caterpillars.

Sometimes the tree is positively buzzing when the blossoms are fully open. Busy bees are at work searching for nectar and transferring pollen from bloom to bloom. Go out after a rainstorm and you will find blossoms dashed to the ground, and drowned bees in little puddles.

Hidden in the pink blossom buds of May, weevils may be eating the heart out of the bud. But how do we know that they're in there? As they gnaw away at the bud it discolours; then when it rains, dirty brown drops hang from the buds. This is a tell-tale sign that the pure blossom is tainted. Protected by the petals, the larvae will eat the stamens and then pupate inside the closed flower.

As summer comes on, thousands of aphids will be sucking the leaves on the tree. Look at a leaf to see who's been sucking at the sap. More and more aphids are produced as the babies can soon produce their own young: a true population explosion.

Look out now for ladybirds which come to feast on the aphids and, finding so many of them, lay their own eggs. Watch for the eggs: little yellow ovals that stand on end. The larvae will soon emerge, gnawing the skin of the egg and then eating other larvae and their eggs as well! They have a real weakness for the aphids and they will stay on a leaf until they have eaten every one. One tiny ladybird can eat 100 a day.

Gnats and aphid bugs are also keen on an aphid meal. But the aphids have their champions – the ants which love to eat the honeydew secreted by them. You can see this sticky substance on the leaves, there for the ants to eat, but they are not content to lick it up: they want it fresh from the aphid. So they tap the creatures' bodies to make them excrete it, and fiercely defend their 'herds' from other predators.

Young weevils will by now have left the buds and be living in the tree, munching leaves. Towards the end of summer they will settle in cracks in bark to spend the winter. The caterpillars prefer to go underground, lowering themselves down on threads, burrowing into the soil to pupate.

Coddling moths may come to lay their eggs in the tree at night. During the day they remain hidden on the tree, but you may be able to see them fluttering about looking for exposed apples on which to lay their eggs. Their larvae will crawl into the apples, head straight for the core and begin eating the pips.

Fully grown sweet apples attract many insects: wasps chew around the hole produced by a worm: flies suck away: ladybirds are attracted by the worms' droppings left behind in the hole. Then, when a few apples begin to fall, other, ground-dwelling creatures can get at them. Woodlice love the damp, soft undersides. Turn a fallen apple over gently and you will find some of these little crustaceans. Ants are attracted by the trickle of juice, and earwigs will be there, too.

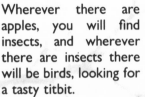

Wherever there are apples, you will find insects, and wherever there are insects there will be birds, looking for a tasty titbit.

Can you find earthworms' holes and see how they pull the apple-tree leaves down into their holes in the ground?

Insects are the favourite food of other animals: hedgehogs and toads enjoy a woodlice snack.

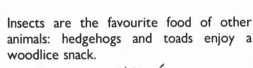

As winter approaches, many birds will enjoy the last of the fallen apples.

And in the dead of winter when all is still and barren, there is life hidden all around the tree, waiting for the warmth of spring; when the creatures emerge and begin eating each other all over again.

BIRDS

I thought the leaves had come to life;
It was the leaf-green birds.

I thought the green leaves
Had found their singing voice —
    the high sweet trill
The tinkling chimes dying away,
The soft zip-zap of earliest spring

A Parliament of Birds John Heath-Stubbs

FLYING VISITORS

What is it about birds that so delights small children? Is it their lively chatter and song, or is it that the concept of flight is so thrilling? It is amazing that, though heavier than air, birds can fly with such ease that all children at some point flap their arms up and down hoping that they, too, will soar into the sky. But children lack the powerful muscles that press the wings downwards, the structure of the wings themselves and the birds' built-in air pockets. Once a bird has taken off, the pressure of the air helps keep it in the air.

Encourage the birds to visit you by letting children feed them. If food is put out regularly, some birds will become used to this and will turn up each time the door or window opens. There are always a few greedy ones who snatch the best bits and fly off with them ... much to the delight of small children who will often shout instructions and advice to the underdogs.

If a feeding routine is established, it is vital to keep at it in winter when the birds may have become dependent on human help. In spring it can be stopped gradually when the birds begin to forage for themselves as nesting begins.

Bread on its own is not nutritious enough as a regular diet. Either buy a seed-mix from a pet shop or make your own. Choose a few of the 'bird recipes' here and put in some garden plants that the birds will appreciate, especially berry-bearing shrubs such as Virginia creeper, mountain ash, holly and ivy.

FEED THE BIRDS

Buy Finch mix for small seed-eating birds and Pigeon mix for larger ones from your local pet shop. Put this out regularly as the birds will become accustomed to it, and may depend on it.

Mix your own

Combine a selection of seeds and cereals, choosing from among wheat, millet, hemp, rape, poppy, linseed, barley, rice and oats.

A bird brush

To offer the birds your seed mixture, try this. Look for a CLEAN old scrubbing brush. Melt some bacon rind or lard in a pot, and dip the brush into the fat. Then sprinkle your seed mix onto it, and, as the fat congeals, the seeds will be fixed to it. Tie the brush to a tree in a spot safe from cats.

Bags of food

Mesh bags, saved from fruit or onions, may be filled with peanuts, maize or another favourite bird food. (One mesh bag inside another reduces the size of the holes.) Tie them together or separately, and hang them in a suitable place. To protect the food from the rain, use a saucer from a plastic flowerpot as a roof. Punch a hole in the saucer and tie it above the nets with plastic wire.

peanuts

maize

sunflower seeds

A piece of cake

Making a seed-cake for birds is easy. Melt some bacon rind, lard or dripping and mix in any of the seeds mentioned in your seed mix recipe, along with dried fruit bits, suet, left-over meat or fish. As it begins to set, wrap it in Saran Wrap and roll it up like a Plasticine sausage about 4 centimetres (1½ inches) in diameter. Cool, then slice it up as you need it. You can also pour the mixture into a yoghurt carton mould with a string set in it for hanging up.

P.S.

Blackbirds like over-ripe apples and apple cores so throw some onto the lawn for them to enjoy...

In winter, drinking water may freeze over, so break the ice for the birds...

Rake over the compost heap to expose the insects that robins like so much...

A CONSTANT WATER SUPPLY

A drinking machine is easily made and ideal for birds in winter when their usual drinking places may be frozen over.

All you need is a plastic cold-drinks bottle, an old saucer, some straw, wire and two pieces of wood.

Fix the two pieces of wood together to make an L-shape. Strong glue will do the trick, but nails or screws may be more secure.

Pierce two holes just below the neck of the bottle.

Fill it with water and put the cap on tightly. Turn it upside down on the saucer: the water will trickle out of the holes and fill the saucer. It won't overflow, because the air pressure exerts a downward force on the water in the saucer and holds up the column of water in the bottle.

Decorate the bottle with straw to cover it up and fix it onto the L-shaped stand with the wire.

Use more wire to tie the drinking machine to a tree. When the birds drink from the saucer, it is constantly refilled from the bottle.

Refill the bottle whenever necessary.

A HOME
OF THEIR OWN

goldfinch

wren

blackbird nest

Birds are inventive, if not always sensible, when it comes to choosing nesting places. They may select a man-made spot for their home, purpose-built nesting boxes, bought or built by a bird lover. Interestingly however, in spite of the luxurious homes offered to them, some birds go for spots that their willing human helpers would never consider suitable – the flowerpot hanging in a macramé swing outside a friend's kitchen window, or ugly, utilitarian shelves for garden tools which provide excellent shelter from rain and winds for a blackbird family.

If you decide to encourage birds to nest in your domain by providing nesting boxes for them, always put them on the south side of trees where there is more protection. A hollow log can make an excellent nesting box, but you can use clay flowerpots or wood, disguised with rafia, straw or bark to make a nesting box look as natural as possible.

'But how do they make nests so well?'

Parents may find themselves trying to explain this amazing skill. How do you explain instinct to a child? Tell your inquisitor that birds are not the brilliant, reasoning architects they seem to be, but rather are

BIRD WATCH

You may want to watch birds more closely than simply keeping an eye out for them in the garden or on a walk. You will need to be concealed, warm and comfortable for quite a long time. (I say this with feeling! I have spent many hours on cold concrete paving, fascinated by the hard-working blackbird parents feeding their helpless young. They were beginning to leave the nest and were quite unable or unwilling to forage for food. Nor would they try to fly despite demonstrations and entreaties from Mum and Dad.)

Wear layers of dull-coloured clothing so that you do not stand out too much. If the day becomes warmer it's easy to slip off a layer and cool down. Chips and other paper-wrapped foods make a noise that will scare the birds away, so you'll have to keep hunger at bay with soggy sandwiches or soft cake!

You'll also need a pair of binoculars and a waterproof jacket, the latter is useful for sitting on when it's not raining.

Build a hide by all means, but sitting still convinces birds that you are no threat. I find that lying on the ground sunbathing or reading convinces many birds that I am safe.

programmed like little computers to produce exactly this sort of nest. Birds build nests by instinct, spiders spin webs and ants built cities all by being programmed to do so. In a short lifespan with survival at a premium, nature has seen to it that creatures will produce the shelter required, without the years of 'trial-and-error' learning or reasoning that we must undergo.

I was once explaining that birds build their nests as a place to lay their eggs, when one child asked whether the birds had little stoves on which to cook these eggs!

MORNING SONG

Early risers will hear the dawn chorus – birds signalling their territory and singing, seemingly, for pure joy. Begin to listen in early spring when there are fewer singers about and you will find it easy to hear the first singers move off to begin looking for food and their place in the dawn chorus gradually taken up by later arrivals. You will also find it easier to differentiate other bird signals – the alarm calls, gentle chattering and cooing and other repeated noises.

GARDENERS' FRIENDS

Birds do a lot more than chatter in the garden! Explain to your child that they help us in many ways as we can appreciate when we watch them closely. Starlings clean up and aerate the lawn; sparrows are busy hunting caterpillars and greenfly for their young; the tiny insects on the twigs of trees are taken by tits; blackbirds devour slugs and thrushes snatch snails.

Distinguishing seed-eaters and insect-eaters

You can tell the difference between the two types by looking at the beaks. Seed-eaters have short, small, strong bills for crunching the seeds: insect-eaters have longer bills so that they can reach into holes when grubbing for their food.

CARING FOR AN INJURED BIRD

Bird experts warn that if you have taken in an injured bird and it does not recover enough to be released into the wild, it will be your responsibility for the rest of its life. So, heartbreaking as it may be, it is often necessary to leave a bird that is so badly injured that it will be unable to fend for itself.

Wild birds should only be kept in captivity if slightly injured or obviously unwell, and then only until they are fit enough to be released.

Birds sometimes fly into glass windows and stun themselves. If you find an unconscious bird keep it in a warm, dark place until it moves and then release it. Call a vet if you think there are any broken bones.

If you find a frozen or injured bird and decide to take it home, put it gently into a cardboard box in which ventilation holes have been punched. A frozen bird should be kept in a warm room, or in a spot beneath a light bulb. Seed-eaters should be offered Finch or Pigeon mix, depending on the size of the bird, and may well appreciate a little fresh or dried fruit, bacon rind, lard or dripping and, of course, fresh water.

As the bird recovers, it will need exercise to prepare for its release. Move it to a new home – a larger box in which perches have been fitted so that it can hop from one to another. Large cardboard supermarket boxes are ideal, especially those made for apples as they have round holes at intervals along the sides. Pieces of dowel pushed through these make the perches. You can cover the holes with pieces of muslin so that the birds can't escape through them.

When the bird is fit and active, take the box into the garden and let the bird fly off.

TREES

Trees ... of virtuous root;
Gem yielding blossoms, yielding fruit,
Choice gums and precious balm;

A Song to David Christopher Smart

LIFE IN A TREE

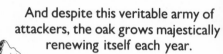

The leaves form the diet of cockchafers and various moth caterpillars: weevil grubs mine the leaves and gall wasps cause gall growths to form on the tree.

Among the bird inhabitants in the oak there could be blue jays, crows and robins, as well as woodpeckers, owls and sparrows among the smaller birds roosting in the trunk. Jays, pigeons and even pheasants love eating the acorns, competing for them with squirrels, mice, voles and rats.

And despite this veritable army of attackers, the oak grows majestically renewing itself each year.

The leaf material on the ground is home to even more animals attracted by the fungi that grow among the roots. Rabbits and hares can be occasionally glimpsed, nibbling acorns. Woodlice live beneath the leaf mould, along with various little grubs that provide a tasty snack for hedgehogs.

One mature tree, an oak for example, can be home to so many creatures, besides children! Life is going on in a complete inter-related fashion in the magic tree, the one in which a child climbs and dreams.

Help him to notice that the tree is home and host to plants, insects and animals. Its bark will support algae, lichens, mosses and fungi. Woodlice will hide under the bark, and ants may send armies up and down it. Insect larvae, caterpillars and aphids feed upon the leaves and these animals in turn become the food of other insects, such as ladybirds and spiders, to say nothing of insect-eating birds which build their nests here and rear their young in the branches.

Be aware, too, of the changing seasons. The buds of spring are followed by the summer growth which gives way to autumn colours and falling leaves. Listen together to the sounds of the wind rustling through the leaves and you will find that the rustle varies from season to season according to the moisture content of the leaves.

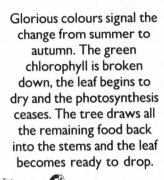

There are two main types of trees. The evergreens are just what their name suggests, shedding and regrowing their leaves continuously, always looking green and covered with leaves. The deciduous trees, including the oak, shed their leaves in winter, leaving bare stems. In spring, they grow new leaves that soon reach full size, completing their life cycle from bud to decay in one year.

Glorious colours signal the change from summer to autumn. The green chlorophyll is broken down, the leaf begins to dry and the photosynthesis ceases. The tree draws all the remaining food back into the stems and the leaf becomes ready to drop.

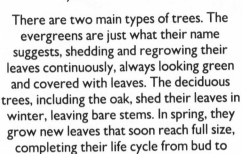

evergreen

deciduous

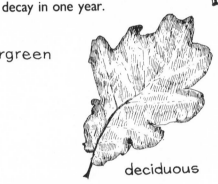

On the ground, the fallen leaves collect in drifts, providing shelter for many living creatures. As the leaves decay, they become humus, a rich nutrient for other living plants.

Leaves wilt and die from lack of water or extreme cold. Without sunlight, the leaves are unable to manufacture food for the tree and are shed. This also cuts down on water evaporating from the leaves.

Life in the litter

Let your child poke around in leaf litter and examine the scurrying creatures he disturbs. There will be woodlice, millipedes, slugs and snails, caterpillars, larvae of various sorts, and mites. He will probably see the earthworms, busy pulling decaying leaf matter into their holes. In autumn, look for long, spindly-legged harvestmen.

Right for the job

Look for examples of deciduous and evergreen trees and collect a leaf from each. Examine them closely with your child to see if there are any special adaptations. Many evergreens have needle-like or waxy leaves to minimize moisture loss. Broad-leaved trees are usually deciduous.

SAPS AND RESINS

Many plants ooze sap and by cutting a stem you and your child can take a closer look at it. Some saps are milky, while others are transparent and gluey. Never let a child taste or touch the sap: many of them are poisonous and some may irritate the skin.

Resins do a valuable job for the plant or tree, protecting them by forming a scab much in the same way that fibrogen in the human blood blocks a wound. This prevents harmful spores from taking hold in the damp, exposed tissue of the broken branch.

All parts of the conifers carry resin which some people think has antiseptic properties. Its value to 'blocked-nose head cold sufferers' is unchallenged when mixed with hot water and the steam used as an inhalant.

Children may want to know about the ways in which man uses saps, resins and gums. Pine resin is an ingredient in paints and varnishes. Gums, secretions from trees and plants that harden in drying but retain their stickiness, are used in the form of glues. The latex of the rubber tree has obvious uses, and many of us have enjoyed maple syrup. A less obvious but fascinating use of sap comes to us from the common dandelion: the sap from its leaves has been used to make rubber. And one enterprising scientist has produced glue from bluebell bulbs.

WATCH IT FLOAT

Examine a cork and determine the direction in which the lenticels run. Then put it in a bowl of water and see how it floats in one position only. If you turn it over, it will right itself and revert to its original position. (Did you know that the man who first thought of putting corks in bottles to keep the contents fresh was a French monk called Dom Perignon?)

SMELLING THE RESIN

Look at the bark of a fir tree. Can you find some blobs or scabs of resin? Scrape them off and drop them into hot water. You will enjoy the clean, fresh smell that is given off, especially if you've got a head cold. If there are no resin blobs, collect some of the needles and infuse them. Your kitchen will smell beautifully.

TREE FARMING

There are many other interesting things to discover about trees, not just for your child! Trees are 'farmed' for a wide variety of products apart from timber, paper and charcoal.

Cork is obtained from the bark of a particular oak. Sheets are peeled off and the tree is rested for seven years, by which time it has replaced the bark and can be stripped again. Because cork contains little pockets of air, called lenticels, it must be cut at right angles to these breathing pores. If it wasn't, air would get through the cork into the contents of the bottle and spoil them, and liquids and gases could escape through. Even with this vertical cut, there is still a little evaporation. French brandy producers call the tiny amount they lose each year through the cork 'the angels' portion.

Cork floats because of the air trapped in these spaces, which also gives cork its insulating properties.

Rubber plantation workers make angular cuts in the bark of the trees, making fresh ones every two or three days, and collect the latex that drips into cans tied under the cuts. Latex from the jelutong tree is used to make chewing gum.

Turpentine is tapped from many species of pine and the acacia trees exude large blobs of gum arabic.

Oils and spices

The essential oils of many trees have their own uses. Eucalyptus oil will clear a stuffy head: sandalwood oil has a heady perfume: Brazil nut oil is used for making margarine, as is palm oil which also crops up in the manufacture of soaps and candles.

We get cloves from the flower bud of *Syzygium aromaticum* and cinnamon is peeled from the inner bark of *Cinnamonum zeylanicum*.

Protective bark

The bark is a protective covering that shields the inner growth with a tough, scaly outer shield.

A tree makes fresh growth under the bark every year which creates the rings that tell us the tree's age — one for every year of growth.

As long as it is alive, the soft living part under the bark goes on growing, channelling sap rather like our blood vessels. So if a ring is cut through the bark, right round the tree, the sap can't rise and the tree dies.

The bark is the home of many animals and tiny plants which can be studied on the spot without harming the tree by stripping off pieces of bark.

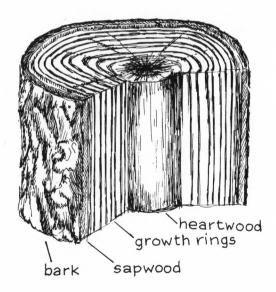

bark · growth rings · sapwood · heartwood

RUB UP
THE RIGHT WAY

Make a rubbing of the bark of a tree by tying a piece of paper around it with string and rubbing over with a wax crayon. (To make a plaster cast, see page 103.)

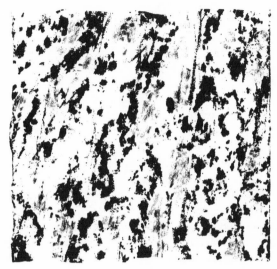

bark pattern
of the oak tree

FAR-REACHING
ROOTS

How far do the roots of a tree extend? To find this out, dig a few holes in radiating circles going outwards from the trunk. Look around and see if the network of roots has affected the vegetation on the ground beneath the tree. If the tree has a large tree canopy, has the shade cast influenced the ways in which the plants around the tree have grown? Try and find some fungi growing among the roots.

OF TREEHOUSES AND MEMORIES

Inside every adult are childhood memories of treehouses, as I have discovered from asking adults at random at school gates and in supermarket queues!

My questions evoked amazing tales of daring and adventure, in private gardens, school playgrounds and in parks. Eyes sparkled and words spilled out from even the most hesitant or curt speaker. They told of games and rituals, passwords and fantasies, but the common thread running through all the reminiscences was the special separateness of this tree-life from the normal world inhabited by adults.

Your understanding of your child's need to have a special hideaway or quiet time alone to dream of Wonderlands and Never-Never-lands is essential. Once you have checked that he is quite safe, keep your distance.

My son installed comfort in his treehouse with a strip of old carpet and a much-prized 'shelf', but these luxuries did nothing to prevent one outsider from falling out of the tree and breaking his leg. Children who climb up regularly develop a routine and for them there is usually little danger, but for the new person brought into the magic circle there is a risk in looking tough and keeping up with the others in a foreign tree. Keep a wary eye on all newcomers, but not so obviously as to spoil the fun.

Abandon any attempt to grow delicate blooms or precious shrubs at the foot of THE tree. Children fall out of trees, drop things out of them and generally trample the surrounding patch while huddled together to discuss gang tactics.

A CASTLE IN THE AIR

Of course, you don't need an actual structure to be the proud owner of a treehouse. It can exist in your imagination as you perch in the fork of a tree. It may be safer for a parent to place a couple of planks in the tree at a secure point to make a platform. Some people make steps from planks up the trunk, but true, self-respecting treehouse owners will scorn all forms of aid, except a rope.

A route down? The whole idea is to get away where adults can't follow ... steps defeat this purpose. But it is important that the occupants of this house have a reasonably safe route down from the eyrie. Going up is always easier than coming down after scaling the heights. If the adults can't get up there, they won't be much help in getting a stuck climber down either.

What you take up What goes up must come down, they say! If you have yanked up a picnic you've got to eat it, or lower it or throw it down, so stick to plastic and paper.

KEEP A TREE DIARY

A journal of life in the tree is fun to keep and fascinating to read.

Draw a plan of your tree. The leaf area forms a canopy and the direction of growth is affected by other trees growing close-by which will influence the amount of light. The wind constantly blowing from one direction will help shape the tree. Is the canopy directly centred over the trunk? If not, why has it grown unevenly?

Make a note of all the inhabitants and what they feed on. Do they live on the tree? Are they regular visitors or just casual passers-by? Does the animal life predominate on the sheltered side?

Lie beneath your tree and study the canopy through a pair of binoculars. Sketch what you can.

In spring collect a leaf each day and press it. After some weeks you will have a record of leaf growth from bud to full-size leaf.

Revealing rings

How old do you think your tree is? Experts can tell a tree's age very accurately by the rings in the trunk that are revealed when a tree is cut down (see the diagram on page 79) but you don't have to take such drastic action to find out how old your tree is. Tree expert Alan Mitchell has calculated that, with a few exceptions, trees have an average of 2·5 centimetres (1 inch) growth for every year. So, a waist measurement of your tree could give you an indication of its age.

This will only be a rough guide, though. A tree's growth may have been held back if it has had to struggle for food and light.

Make some rubbings or pressings to keep in your diary (see Finds) or preserve the leaves and flowers in its pages (see Plant Crafts).

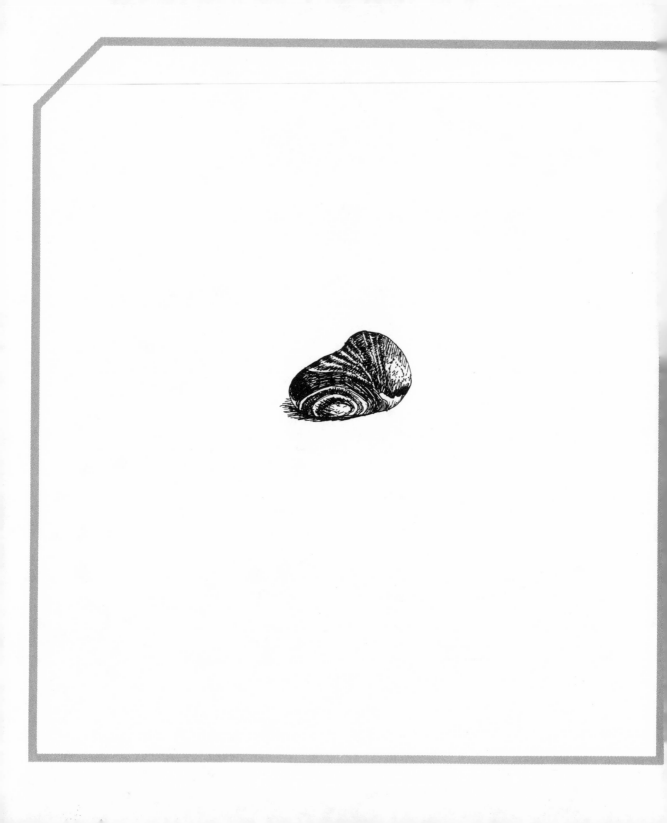

FINDS

Crowding this beach
are milkstones, white
teardrops; flints
edged out of flinthood
into smoothness chafe
against grainy ovals,
pitted pieces, nosestones,
stoppers and saddles;
veins of orange
inlay black beads:
chalk-swaddled babyshapes,
tiny fists, facestones
and facestone's brother
skullstone, roundheads
pierced by a single eye,
purple finds, all
rubbing shoulders:
a mob of grindings,
groundlings, scatterings
from a million necklaces
mined under sea—hills,
    the pebbles
are as various as the people.

Stone speech Charles Tomlinson

FINDS

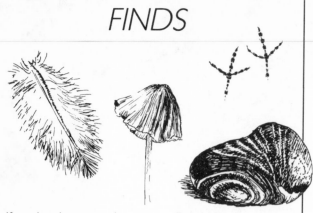

If you're the type who must walk briskly, don't stop here, turn the page and read another section. This is for those parents whose children take an age to walk a few yards, stopping to investigate every little stone and ant along the path. Most kids start off like this: a quick walk to the shops with a toddler can take an hour. In some cases we kill off this curiosity by getting them to hurry all the time, but a few manage to make it into adulthood clinging to this enquiring view.

This section is concerned with oddments which are simply 'found' somewhere, on a walk or in a garden, even on the pavement. But it's not all that haphazard you see: an interest in, say, leaves, could lead to a steady seeking, a planned foray, resulting in triumphal returns to the collection with just the perfect specimen. Very satisfying, provided you are the sort of parent who is prepared to house the 'finds'. Well, I know that some of the amazing items brought back are not the sort of things you would like to live cheek by jowl with, but there are plenty of tolerable collections, and some both fascinating and beautiful.

This calls for long term concentration if you want to carry a project through: for example, the life cycle of a leaf would be stretched out over a year, albeit in short bursts. But there are others which are the work of a moment – finding a perfect piece of driftwood needs no more than the act of discovery and lugging it home.

The ideas suggested here are no more than that, intended to trigger off your own original and personal collections.

LEAVES

Just as we can be identified by our fingerprints, so plants can be distinguished by their leaves which have endless variations of shape, texture, colour and thickness.

The shape of leaves tells us what kind of plant they come from. Some shapes are used as symbols the world over. The shamrock is associated with Ireland: the maple leaf brings Canada to mind. The olive symbolizes peace, while laurel leaves adorn the heads of winners.

Make a leaf collection with a child and you will come across a variety of leaves, each designed for a purpose. There may be palmate, needle-like, three-, four- or five-fingered or star-shaped leaves in your collection of finds. There is a reason for their design and skilful construction, adapting the tree for life in particular conditions.

Each leaf has two distinct sides which are quite dissimilar. You may find silvery undersides and waxy uppers. Notice that the veins are more exposed on the underside. Counting both sides of the leaves, an established tree has an enormous leaf surface.

VITAL CHLOROPHYLL

The dark green surface contains chlorophyll with which a leaf magically uses the power of sunlight to synthesize (combine) the air it breathes with the water and mineral salts it absorbs, producing sugars and starches to feed itself. The undersides are breathing through tiny pores. During the night they give out oxygen and the moisture that refreshes our atmosphere. Strange to think that, as the leaves ripple and twirl in the breeze, all this is going on at the same time. Leaves make different sounds in the wind. Some rustle, others whisper. Stop, listen with your child and try to distinguish sounds coming from certain trees.

Have a look at the way the leaves are joined to the trees as this affects the way they react to currents of air. Some poplars, for example, ripple even on a seemingly airless day.

Leaf designs are adapted to their environment. Pine needles enable them to survive in dry conditions, while water lilies have huge, flat leaves that are designed to float.

BURSTING BUDS

In deciduous trees the leaves lie curled up in protective buds over the winter. Then, with the rising sap and the warmth of spring, the buds swell and the tiny leaves burst out and unfurl in the weak sunshine. As the weather becomes warmer, the leaves grow rapidly, working all the time during summer, and when autumn comes they fade, dry and fall. Rains dissolve the leaves into skeletal traces of veins and stems, then decay sets in and they return to the earth, breaking down into their component elements, enriching the forest floor and nourishing plant life.

autumn leaf falling

LEAF COLLECTING

Shapes
Collect the leaves from different trees and look at them carefully to appreciate their variations and try to find out reasons for the differences.

Seasonal cycle
Take them when they have just budded and at the various stages of growth right through to the rusty, fallen leaves of autumn and you will see the life cycle for yourself.

LEAFY RECORDS

Preserve your finds by . . .

Rubbing
Lay the leaf face down on a sheet of card and cover it with a sheet of paper. Rub evenly with a wax crayon and an impression of the leaf will come through. Rubbing will work well with leaves that are not too delicate with strongly defined veins.

Making a silhouette
Lay your specimen on a sheet of paper and paint with steady strokes from just inside the edge of the leaf onto the paper. When you have painted all round the leaf, take it off the paper and you will find a perfect record of its shape.

Printing
Leaf prints can be made by brushing shoe polish over the leaf and pressing onto paper, polished side down. Capture the colours of autumn by using the brown, red and amber tints now available.

Pressing
Lay the leaf between sheets of blotting paper or paper towel and layer several sheets of newspaper over this. Top with a heavy weight; a few telephone books or a couple of bricks will do the trick. Leave for three weeks.

FOUND FEATHERS...

Interesting feathers may come your way on a walk or in a garden. Your child may admire them simply for their beauty, from soft fluffy down to silky technicolour, but feathers have had other purposes and meanings for man which a child could use as a game.

Trying to write with a feather quill is a must in these days of ballpoint pens. The scratchy effort seems laborious to us but is hilarious to children. Quills were generally made from goose quills, sharpened with a knife. Other parts of the feathers can be used for

making patterns and designs with ink. Cut the tip of the feathers into geometric shapes – triangles, diamonds or chevrons – and print with these.

Examine a typical feather together and you will see it has a horny shaft and a flat vane. The vane is rather like a comb with fine barbs linked to one another with hook-like barbules. These reassemble the vane smoothly if stroked and this is exactly what a bird does when preening. Look at these little hooks under a magnifying glass and see the joining zip-like action working.

Can your child tell which are tail feathers and which are flight or down feathers?

Feathers can be most easily found in early spring and mid-summer when the birds are moulting.

... MAKE FINE BRAVES

To Indian braves, the feathers spoke a language. Each feather in the head-dress was a symbol speaking to others of the bravery and fighting history of the wearer. Feathers were earned in battle and worn like school colours.

A few strands of red-dyed horsehair (use cotton thread) tied into the top of a feather meant that the brave had killed an enemy. A red feather notched meant that he had scalped an enemy, whilst a feather split or dyed red meant that the poor fellow had been wounded.

The position of the feather had significance. If it stood straight up, it meant 'brave deed': if tilted it meant 'less brave deed': and a feather pointing straight down meant 'least brave deed' – still brave, mind you, just not very brave!

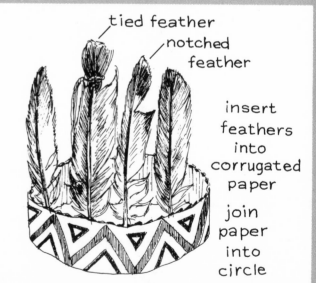

tied feather

notched feather

insert feathers into corrugated paper

join paper into circle

Devise your own feather language – a perfect signalling code.

PAINTING STONES

The easiest stones to paint on are those which are smooth, flat and not too small. The ideal place to find them is near water in rivers or on beaches, for the constant pounding of the water will have smoothed the stones perfectly for you.

Scrub them with hot soapy water and let them dry thoroughly. Use a pencil to draw designs on them, or to scratch on your pattern. Then colour the design with oil or acrylic paints – water colour and poster paints will wash off, and do not have the density of colour needed for good effects. Modellers' enamel paint is also suitable.

Use good quality brushes or pens, or even sticks of reed and feather quills. When the design is finished and the paint dry, coat the stone with polyurethane varnish. Remember to wash out the brushes with white spirit, which is also handy for cleaning up any mess.

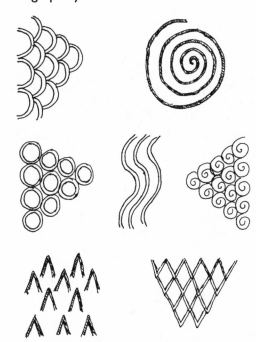

STUNNING STONES

Smooth, water-washed pebbles often suggest ideas for painting animals or fish shapes on them. Some are simply so beautiful that they need no decoration: they can be kept just as they are. The feel of these smooth stones in the hand leads many children to keep a favourite stone in a pocket, as you will find when turning out trousers for washing. Collecting pebbles on a beach or riverbank is irresistible, but children find them in the least likely places. Precious and treasured objects – so easily obtained.

SILKEN WEBS

To see magical, silvery webs, go into the garden with children early on a misty morning and the fragile, delicate threads are suddenly outlined, glistening with minute droplets that reveal their perfect symmetry. Sometimes, webs are made visible by the drops of a sprinkler, but for a large part of the day we barely see them.

Tiny, sheet webs cover lawns: hammock webs, thick sheets of silk, conceal the spider waiting beneath them, but it is the vertically rigged orb webs of the garden spider that hang like networks of diamonds.

These symmetrical masterpieces are destroyed by wind, rain or sudden movement, and the spiders efficiently reconstruct them along a pre-arranged defined pattern.

In fact, the spider retraces the design twice. The first web is simply a foothold created from non-sticky thread which the spider walks around a second time, eating it as she spins sticky silk behind her for the final web.

The spider is constantly aware of the tension of the web and is alert to the slightest movement in it. She will know at once if the tiniest mite is caught.

The Zygiella spider leaves out the cross threads from two sections of the web and waits under a leaf with a leg on the radial thread, ready to rush out and deal with anything caught in the web.

Expect someone to ask 'Why doesn't the spider stick to her own web?' She has an oily secretion on her feet that prevents her sticking to the threads, and, besides, the webs are generally intended for catching creatures weaker than the spider. If a huge insect gets enmeshed in the web, the spider simply sits still, waiting for it to break free before repairing her spun trap, which she can cut if she needs to.

In proportion to its weight, the spider's web is extraordinarilly strong. Weight for weight, it would work out stronger than steel cable! The spiders themselves are strong in relation to their size.

'How does the spider build its web?'

The first thing she must do is find two supports and then sling a line between them. This is easy if the web is in a position where the spider can simply walk around to the second point from the first, unreeling her silk as she goes. But if the two are disconnected, like little twigs some distance apart, she lets out a length of silk and waits for the wind to carry it across the gap and entangle her line around the twig.

Next, she lets out a loose thread, and from the centre of it drops another to form the stem of a 'Y'-shape. Then she attaches the end of this third thread to

WEB WATCHING

Next time you spot a web, make a drawing of it that shows the size and design. If you take your sketch pad back a day or two later you may notice whether or not the spider has enlarged her catchnet area by adding new sections around the original: rather like humans, building extensions to their houses.

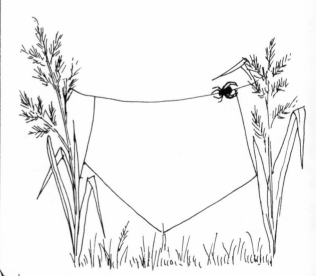

GO CATCH A WEB

A light puff of talcum powder blown onto a web will settle on the threads and outline it perfectly. This will give you a clear view of the web. You can actually catch them and glue them onto card. To do this, first of all dust some talc onto the web which makes it easily seen against dark paper. Spray the surface of the paper, or card with Spraymount, an adhesive glue which emits a fine, sticky mist. Approach the web, holding the mount at the same angle, essential for getting the web onto the mount intact. When the web is stuck onto the card, spray it with a fixative and you can take it home and study the amazing structure at your leisure.

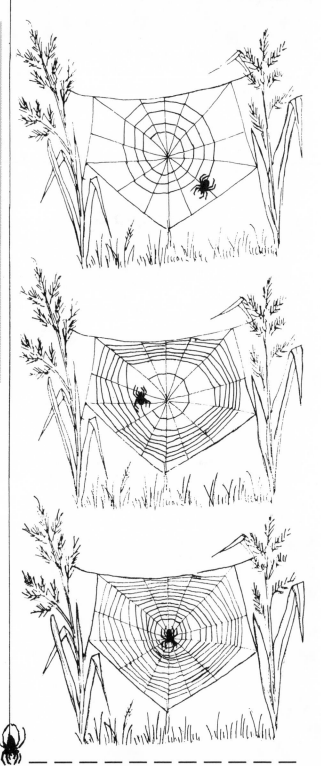

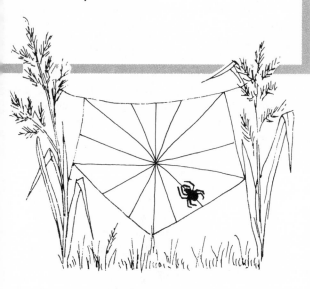

another support. Gradually she adds more threads, radiating outwards from the join of the 'Y' until she completes the wheel-like frame. In the centre she makes herself a little platform. Next, working outwards from the centre platform in a spiral, she lays the first web which she will later destroy as she spins her second, sticky spiral.

CONES

Stop and gather some cones while on a walk. The large, beautiful ones strewn beneath the tree are the females: the males are usually smaller. The males produce pollen which is carried, often great distances, on the wind and lands on a female cone. It can take a year or more to grow in and fuse with the cell inside, and two more years may pass before the cone is mature and the seeds ripe for dispersal. The cones gradually swell and become woody as the seeds develop between the scales.

The seeds have a tiny wing, so that once they are mature they can fly to a suitable spot to germinate in the soil.

If the seeds were to be released in damp, rainy weather they would land in a soggy heap at the bottom of the tree. To avoid this, the cones are designed to open when the weather is dry and the seeds can take to the air.

AN OPEN AND SHUT CASE

Put a selection of cones, some open others closed, in a plastic bag with a little water in it. Keep this in a moist place. Put a similar selection in a dry warm corner. You will notice that the first cones have detected the moisture in the air and will close, while those in the warm, dry spot will open.

Cones are worth studying for their beauty alone. The designs on the scales, which are a type of leaf, vary and the colour and texture are remarkably different. Drawing a pile of cones in a basket helps you to observe their individual characteristics.

FUNGI

Puffballs contain millions of spores which are shot out in clouds. Stinkhorns release their spores in a smelly fluid that attracts flies which carry the spores away with them.

Look under the cap of a typical toadstool and you will see the spore pattern, either on radiating gills or on linings of numerous tubes from which they can drop, to be carried away by the wind.

Take a look with your child at a typical toadstool or mushroom and you will see that there is no green colouring present. This is because fungi contain no chlorophyll to make their food. Instead, they absorb it from their surroundings, leaf mould, logs and twigs. The fungi send fine, silken threads deep down into other plants to the layer of food matter. The parts that you see are the reproductive areas.

MAKE A SPORE PRINT

The umbrella-type of fungi are the most suitable for prints. Avoid all poisonous varieties. (These are identified in any of the numerous field guides around.) Fungi with white gills print well on dark paper, while those with black ones show up better on light paper.

Pick and handle the toadstool very gently. Cut away the stem flush with the rim and place the fungus, gills down, on a sheet of paper. Cover it with an inverted bowl or jar to prevent draughts affecting your print. After a little time, the spores will have been released onto the paper, making a perfect image. Some release enough spores for a good print in an hour, others release theirs more slowly and need to be left overnight. A toadstool of the same type, similarly cut and placed on a

spore print

sheet of paper but left uncovered can be lifted at intervals to check the release rate. Don't leave your 'printing' cap too long as the definition of the lines is lost and the ridges of the spores fall in and smudge. Make the print permanent by spraying with fixative spray (hair lacquer can be used for black prints) and remember that bracket fungi, puffballs and stinkhorns are unsuitable.

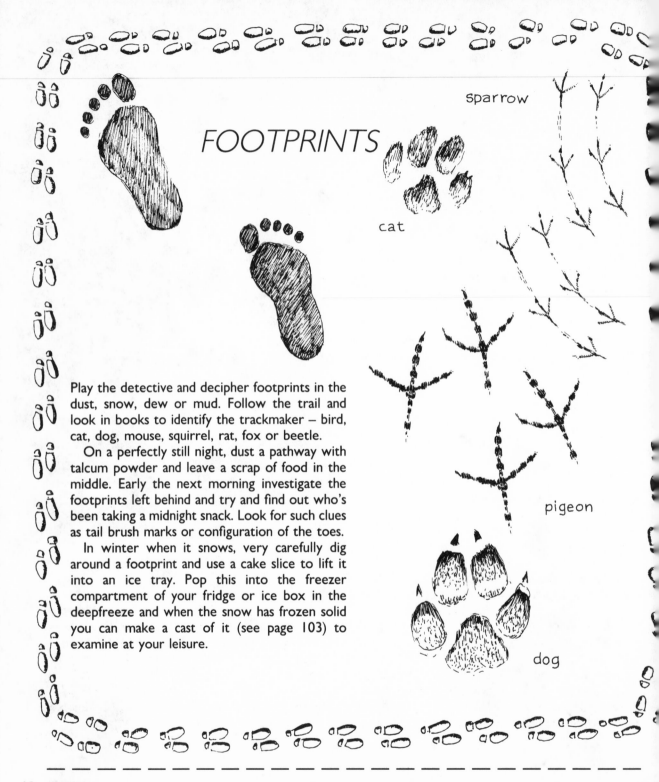

FOOTPRINTS

sparrow

cat

pigeon

dog

Play the detective and decipher footprints in the dust, snow, dew or mud. Follow the trail and look in books to identify the trackmaker – bird, cat, dog, mouse, squirrel, rat, fox or beetle.

On a perfectly still night, dust a pathway with talcum powder and leave a scrap of food in the middle. Early the next morning investigate the footprints left behind and try and find out who's been taking a midnight snack. Look for such clues as tail brush marks or configuration of the toes.

In winter when it snows, very carefully dig around a footprint and use a cake slice to lift it into an ice tray. Pop this into the freezer compartment of your fridge or ice box in the deepfreeze and when the snow has frozen solid you can make a cast of it (see page 103) to examine at your leisure.

NATURE'S DEBRIS

There are other objects simply lying around that will captivate the curious. A broken egg shell suggests that somewhere in the trees above a fledgling is being fed by its mother. A deserted bird's nest can be studied for its clever construction. A group of empty snail shells may mark a thrush's anvil. Cones may show the gnawing marks made by squirrels. Footprints and droppings can indicate who has been here before. Looking at nature's debris through a child's eyes is an experience that can enhance our perception of the ordinary.

With a little luck, while out on a walk along the seashore, or a ramble by a river, your child may come upon a piece of driftwood that has a graceful shape. If he brings it home he can wax it gently with a soft cloth to bring out the texture of the wood. It may suggest some natural form, as a perfect piece of natural sculpture or it may complement some grouped stones or dried material.

PLANT CRAFTS

I too will something make
And Joy in the making.

Robert Bridges

ARRANGING FLOWERS

Age is no factor in determining who enjoys arranging flowers, nor is gender. Even a toddler loves admiring 'his flowers' when he's arranged them in his own way.

Children often pick plants on a walk and come home triumphant with a mixed bunch of wilted leaves. It is important to explain early on to a child that some plants are rare and others poisonous, so we can't simply gather indiscriminately. That said, there are many plants that may be picked and admired indoors.

When to pick

Gather the blooms early in the morning, or better still in the late afternoon. Take a basket with you or gently lay them on the lawn until cutting is complete. If you are cutting a lot at once, stand them in a can of water in the shade with the water right up to their necks as flowers are thirstiest when freshly picked. Always cut the stems at an angle, never straight across.

Any leaves that will be below the waterline in the final arrangement should be trimmed off because they rot and hasten the deterioration of the flowers.

Roses should be immersed in water at once and the end centimetre of the stems snipped off underwater. Wear gloves when handling roses as you have to remove some of the larger thorns. Use a thorn stripper if you have one: if not, gently push your thumb against the flat side of the thorn and break it off.

Woody stems should be bashed or slashed and bark peeled back; oozing stems should be singed for a moment to seal them. Daffodils can be slit at the bottom of the stem to make them last longer.

Making it last

When the arrangement is complete, the water level should be topped up. Some plants enjoy a teaspoon of sugar added to the water, especially those with petals that are inclined to droop quickly. Tulips firm up and hang onto their petals fiercely with this treatment.

A teaspoon of cut flower preservative food is helpful, too. Alum is often used for hydrangeas, and decay can be kept at bay with a squirt of soap or drop of antiseptic added to the water.

The finished masterpiece should not be put in a draught or on a window ledge that gets direct sunshine. Spots above radiators or other direct heat sources should also be avoided.

Arrangements can be made more interesting by using twigs, bark, seed heads or huge leaves, and if any flower heads are knocked off their stems they can be floated in a bowl of water where their upturned beauty is offered to our gaze.

KEEP IT SIMPLE

Choose your container with some thought for how the final arrangement will look, where it will stand and what flowers you are using. Simple forms complement the flowers best. Universal glass cylinders show everything off to perfection and you will get much pleasure from looking at the stems, especially of tulips. Pottery has a natural feel and so does wicker, while old copper jugs give the flowers a mellow glow.

Very young flower arrangers should be content with a simple vase, arranging just a few stems to begin with. You can also use a bowl fitted with Oasis floral foam fixed firmly with tape so that it can be reused several times. It's great fun sticking a stem into this, seeing how it looks and adjusting it if necessary.

Wired vases are for older children, and if you're using one, make sure that the chicken wire crumpled in the bowl is wedged firmly. You'll probably find a florist's rose quite hard to cope with, but if you are intent on trying to use one, fix it to the bottom with waterproof putty.

CHAINS OF ENCHANTMENT

It is a small step from making simple daisy chains to creating elaborate garlands. Your child can feel like a fairy queen – and so can any pets who find themselves crowned and garlanded.

In summer, when daisies carpet the grass, look for tall, strong-stemmed ones to pick. Show children how to slit through the stem with your fingernail a little way down from the flower and insert the stem of the next one, and so on until a floral chain has been forged.

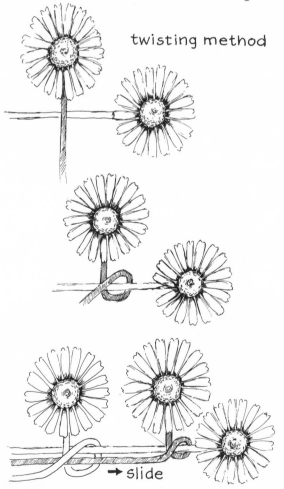

twisting method

→ slide

ENTWINING AND TWISTING

You can use the twisting method to create a garland of clover, daisies, scabiosa, grasses and other plants with pliant, flexible green stems. Put two stems at right angles to each other and twist the stem of the vertical one under the horizontal stem, and then over and along as shown in the drawing. Build up your garland adding flowers and foliage in this way until a ring is formed, and then twist the ends in to secure them.

LOOPING THE LOOPS

When you have lovely, trumpet-shaped flowers on inflexible stems, strip them carefully from the stems and make a garland using the string method illustrated here. Tie soft string into a loop as shown, keeping one end loose. With this, you secure the trumpets into the loop made by the other two strings and you will soon have a glorious garland.

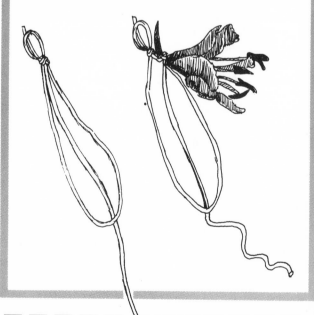

PRESSED BEAUTY

Pressing is an utterly simple yet magical way to capture one glorious autumn leaf or a perfect violet.

Look at the shape and shading of individual petals with children; they may remind you of other shapes. If petals are being collected for pressing, ideas will crowd into the imagination – butterfly wings in pansy patterns or goldfish tails in split tulip petals.

As the seasons change, the altering colours and textures of leaves can be recorded by pressing.

A PRESSED-FLOWER WINDOW PICTURE

A translucent picture hung in a window where the light will shine through the pressed petals is easy to make. Build up a picture with pressed flowers, using flexible vinyl (clear plastic sold in rolls in art and hardware stores) as the backing board. It is easy to cut into any shape you like. Stick the petals on to it with clear adhesive or eggwhite and cover the finished picture with prepared acetate, a clear adhesive sheet.

Children can create sensitive pictures either of flowers or fantasy subjects. Small fragments suggest animal or insect shapes … a butterfly might emerge, made from the antennae-like fuchsia stamens and wing-shaped tulip pieces with pansy 'eyes' overlaid on them. Honeysuckle buds become insect bodies.

Reds and blues don't press particularly well, but buttercups retain the bright yellow of trapped sunshine, and autumn leaves, being already partially dry, retain their colour well.

card
covered
with
acetate

MARK THE PLACE WITH PRESSED FLOWERS

Flower presses are cheap and easily available, but just as good are old telephone books and other heavyweight tomes that have been gathering dust for ages. The method is the same whatever form of press you use.

Put the plant material between two sheets of absorbent paper, pop this sandwich between the pages of the book and close it. Put a few more heavy books on top and leave the flower to dry for at least four weeks.

These dried leaves and flowers being quite flat can be stuck to card or between sheets of Cellophane to make a delicate and imaginative picture.

Fix the flowers to the Cellophane with egg white which dries transparent: and cover those glued to card with a prepared acetate sheet. Use your card as a pretty bookmark or give it to a keen gardener as a gift.

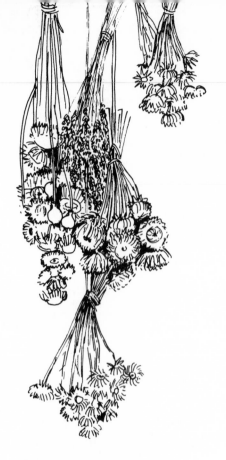

Children can become more aware of the structure of plants when handling them in unusual ways.

Drying allows us to catch and keep the beauty of the season's blooms and enjoy them for many months. In the process of drying, the flowers take on new qualities: some change or lose colour allowing them to be placed in an arrangement with new companions that would be incompatible in the living flush of sometimes too vibrant colour.

Experimenting together with the various methods, you will find which one is the most suitable for the types of flowers you have. Always dry more than you need: some are inevitably unsatisfactory.

ARTFUL ARRANGEMENTS

Dried flowers, having lost their translucency and very often their leaves, but having become rigid and delightfully delicate, require thoughtful arranging to bring out their true beauty. Children can insert them into florist's foam or a fine wire support to anchor them securely. Show them how to pack flowers tightly to conceal the bare stems and fill any gaps with dried foliage and grasses to form a massed group. Reveal their subtle colours by placing them where the light falls on them from the front or from above. The texture of the arrangement – a strong part of its beauty – can be shown off by choosing a suitable container. Dried flowers have an affinity for natural materials such as wicker baskets or pottery jugs. Tall, graceful grasses and pods look fragile and interesting in tall glass containers which allow the attractive stems to be seen.

I love a tightly packed basket placed on the floor so that we can look down on the densely massed faces of the flowers which always look better if similar colours are crammed together. Haphazard, spotty schemes seem to emphasize the slightly washed out look of some dried flowers.

The list on page 126 suggests which plants lend themselves to the various methods.

EVERLASTING BEAUTY

That elusive quality, eternal youth, is not present in nature's cycle of growth and decay. But drying flowers, seeds and grasses gives them a new permanence. No longer young, turgid and fleshy, they take on a new delicacy of faded form and texture.

Experimenting with drying flowers opens our eyes to plant material normally ignored. Dried flower addicts look at everything to weigh up its potential: and when dried-out seed heads are cut down or thrown on the compost heap they will ask, 'Is there an exciting shape or texture that suggests an arrangement?'

THERE FOR THE TAKING

The simplest way to enjoy dried plants in the house is to collect naturally dried material. In autumn, there is an abundance of this around, as seed heads dry out and leaves lose their moist greenery. Look for branches, bark, bracken, reeds, wheat, hops and grasses.

Air drying

To air dry, gather bunches of material and sort them into small bundles. Strip leaves and fasten each bundle with an elastic band. If the bundles are too large, the plants in the middle will remain too moist. As the material dries, the bundle will shrink: this is why the elastic band is vital. Hang the bundles upside down to give straight stems. If you prefer curving stems, stand the plants in a container so that the stems curve gently outwards. Goldenrod, poppyseed pods, hops and grasses do well with this method because they are not too fleshy to start with.

Sand drying

This efficient and ancient method calls for clean, white sand that can be kept for reuse. Sandpit sand, fine builder's sand and silver sand from gardening centres can be used — even ordinary beach sand works, but this will need to be washed and dried to remove dirt, salt and debris.

Wind wire round the stems as they are not strong enough to support the flower heads. Pour a layer of sand into a shoe box and gently place the wired flowers into it, face down in some cases. Gradually sift the remaining sand onto the flowers until they are fully covered. Leave the box in a warm, dry place until drying is complete. The time will vary according to how moist the flowers were and where you have the container, so have a 'test flower' in a corner of the box so that you can check the progress without disturbing the others.

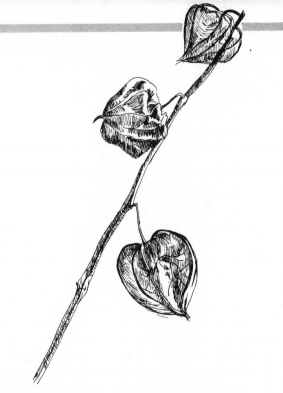

Glycerine

This method is best suited for large sprays of foliage as the leaves remain pliable, look moist and often a little shiny, although the colours may darken. Mix a solution of glycerine — one part glycerine to three parts hot water — and put this into a jar. Slash the ends of the branches from the bottom up a little way and put them into the solution. You may have to support the leaves and top up the solution as it becomes absorbed. As soon as the leaves begin to darken, remove the branches from the jar and hang them upside down in a dark, dry cupboard to complete the drying process.

Storing dried flowers

Glue some florist's foam (Oasis) into the bottom of a large, cardboard box and carefully set the flowers to be stored into it. Cover the box and wrap plastic around it to keep it moisture free. Store in a dark place.

FROM TOUCHING
TO SEEING

There are ways in which we can make visual records of a tactile surface – a translation to picture form of what we experience through our sense of touch. Offer children these three easy techniques and some exciting pictures will be made. You can make a simple print, take an imprint, or take a rubbing of an article to read its texture in visual language.

This activity leads to the discovery of many strange surfaces. It may be a dishcloth or the wrought iron gates passed every day, but recorded in this way it is like seeing it for the first time. Lively awareness is vital for creative thinking, so is curiosity, and children have plenty of that. Once you teach them these simple techniques they'll be taking prints of everything from the soles of their boots to the brick in the wall, not forgetting their fingers and soles of their feet.

leaf prin

prints
from
cauliflower
and
mushroom

Printing

A print can be made by painting or inking a object, then pressing it onto paper or fabric leaving a printed impression. Effective print on fabric or paper can record feathers leaves, sliced vegetables (onion layers yiel stripes), bark, stones and ferns. Stick fragil objects onto a block made from a piece o wood, a matchbox or a cotton spool: th makes them easier to handle and prolong their printing power.

Print fabrics with permanent printing ink such as cold-water dye (non-toxic); un bleached calico is suitable. Follow the instruc tion on the dye container which tell you t put a piece of old fabric – old shirts o pyjamas are ideal – over the print and pres with a hot iron.

When printing on paper, use poster paint powder paint or acrylic and print on slightly coarse, absorbent paper. Experiment with colours: as I write cobalt blue leaf prints on crimson paper adorn the wall behind my typewriter.

feather
print

leaf
rubbings

rubbing
from
sweetcorn

Taking an imprint

For this you need Plasticine, or Playdough, or you can make your own modelling dough by making a smooth paste with 1 cup of plain flour, ½ a cup of salt, 1 tablespoon of vegetable oil and 2 teaspoons of cream of tartar. Cook this in a pan until a ball forms. Keep it in a container with a tightly fitting lid. Imprints can be taken of rough surfaces by pressing any of these materials onto the chosen object to yield a moulded impression. For a temporary but quick result, press the dough against the object, pushing it firmly all over. When pulled away, there will be an impression on the dough.

For a more permanent cast, say the bark of a tree, mould the dough around the bark and tap it firmly all over by holding a flat board against it and hammering it evenly. Remove the dough gently and curve it into a boat shape and form extra endpieces to complete the mould. Make up some Plaster of Paris according to the instructions on the packet and pour it into the mould. When it is firmly set, remove the mould and scrub the cast clean.

There's the rub

Move a wax crayon evenly back and forth on paper laid on the surface you wish to record. The raised areas will be revealed in the rubbing, which can be made from everyday surfaces. You can even make a tree bark rubbing if you tie the paper round the tree with string (see page 79). There's texture on cut logs or plants, manhole covers, leaves, twigs, garden urns, chair seats, tables, gates, netting, rocks and cork to name but a few. The world is yours for the rubbing.

SEED JEWELLERY AND COLLAGE

Seeds are a vast source of ornamental material that we can use to create artistic and natural jewellery. At the same time, simply handling the seeds enables us to marvel at the range and diversity of design. Nature's inventiveness at packaging the precious beginnings of new life is a study in itself.

A glance at the chart on page 106 will give some ideas of the colours you can hope to find.

Beware of a baby also admiring this range of interesting items to put in his mouth. Some may be poisonous, and many could choke a small toddler. From six years old and onwards, however, this is a rewarding and creative hobby that encourages the child to look more closely at how plants reproduce. On a simple level, necklaces are satisfying and attractive to wear. Key rings can be made from one large seed, or a small closed cone. Spray on some shellac and attach the seed or cone to the key ring with powerful adhesive.

Some seeds are gathered from the garden or on a walk: others may be bought from a supermarket or a health shop, not forgetting convenient seed packets in garden departments, fruit pips and bird mixes.

Collage design

The simplest designs are often the most effective – repeat patterns and striking geometrics, diamonds and squares like a patchwork quilt: rows of different types of bean setting off one another, creating stripes, spirals and zigzags, Themes from nature may be tried, woodgrains and leaf patterns, and of course, if translucent grains like rice are being used, colour painted on the cardboard will shine through for special effects like water ripples or glowing jewel-like patterns.

SEED COLLAGE

Sort the seeds into piles of different colours, sizes and markings. You will notice how even seeds of the same plants can vary: the sunflower seed, for example, can be almost black or light and some are zebra-striped.

Enjoy the feel of the seeds while you're doing this and be careful not to allow any younger children to pop them into their mouths, and don't be tempted yourself. Work at a table and use empty egg boxes for sorting the seeds.

Once you've organized the seeds, find a piece of cardboard – a box, the back of a writing pad or the stiff paper inside new shirts will be quite suitable – and draw a picture on it with a pencil.

Now gather together pins, tweezers, a brush, some glue, a spatula and varnish, and spread some newspaper over a work-table.

Some of the most successful designs are made from a small selection of seeds of a similar type.

Large patches of one type contrast nicely with patches or lines made with seeds of different textures or colours. Some dark seeds make good outlines, rather like a stained-glass window or mosaic.

Arrange the chosen seeds loosely to see how they look together, using the spatula to move them around.

Cover a small area of the cardboard with transparent glue (rubber cement which comes with its own brush, and Elmer's Glue-All are good). Dip the tip of a pencil into the glue very lightly to pick up individual seeds and put them into position. Always cover the glued area before moving on to another patch.

When the picture is finished, shake loose any seeds that are not firmly attached and blow away any loose husks, then varnish it. Use colourless nail vanish for small pictures and Polyurethane for larger ones as it's cheaper.

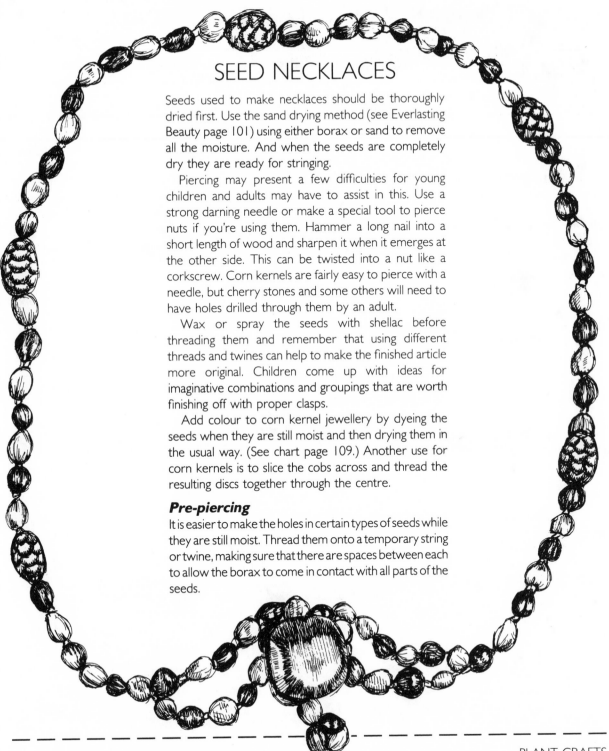

SEED NECKLACES

Seeds used to make necklaces should be thoroughly dried first. Use the sand drying method (see Everlasting Beauty page 101) using either borax or sand to remove all the moisture. And when the seeds are completely dry they are ready for stringing.

Piercing may present a few difficulties for young children and adults may have to assist in this. Use a strong darning needle or make a special tool to pierce nuts if you're using them. Hammer a long nail into a short length of wood and sharpen it when it emerges at the other side. This can be twisted into a nut like a corkscrew. Corn kernels are fairly easy to pierce with a needle, but cherry stones and some others will need to have holes drilled through them by an adult.

Wax or spray the seeds with shellac before threading them and remember that using different threads and twines can help to make the finished article more original. Children come up with ideas for imaginative combinations and groupings that are worth finishing off with proper clasps.

Add colour to corn kernel jewellery by dyeing the seeds when they are still moist and then drying them in the usual way. (See chart page 109.) Another use for corn kernels is to slice the cobs across and thread the resulting discs together through the centre.

Pre-piercing
It is easier to make the holes in certain types of seeds while they are still moist. Thread them onto a temporary string or twine, making sure that there are spaces between each to allow the borax to come in contact with all parts of the seeds.

SEEDS OF MANY COLOURS, LARGE AND SMALL

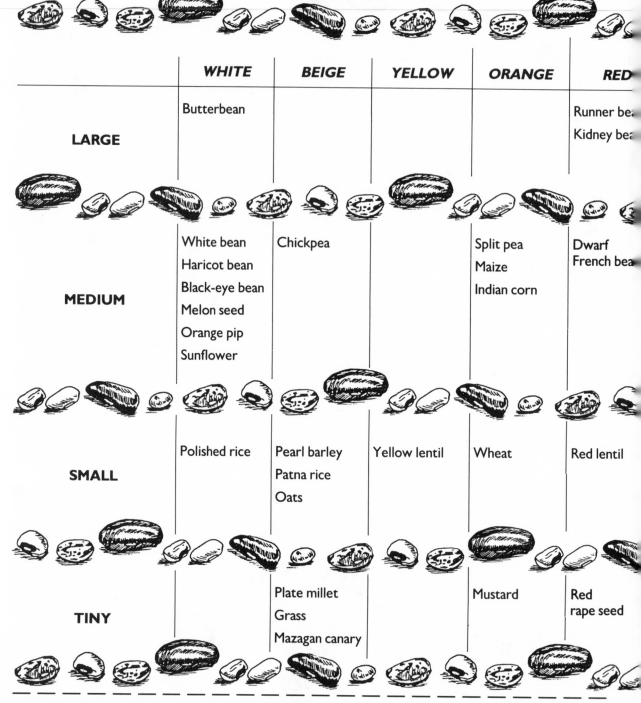

	WHITE	BEIGE	YELLOW	ORANGE	RED
LARGE	Butterbean				Runner bean Kidney bean
MEDIUM	White bean Haricot bean Black-eye bean Melon seed Orange pip Sunflower	Chickpea		Split pea Maize Indian corn	Dwarf French bean
SMALL	Polished rice	Pearl barley Patna rice Oats	Yellow lentil	Wheat	Red lentil
TINY		Plate millet Grass Mazagan canary		Mustard	Red rape seed

LIGHT BROWN	MID-BROWN	DARK BROWN	GREEN	BLUE	GREY	BLACK
			Pumpkin		Sunflower (striped)	Sunflower Dwarf French bean
	Maple pea Gunga bean Rose calop bean	Coffee bean Cow pea Pimento Apple pip	Dried pea Green lentil			
White peppercorn Parsnip	Buckwheat Hollyhock Red lentil		Yellow lentil		Hemp	Tare Black peppercorn
Sesame	Teazle Linseed White cummin			Maw (Poppy seed)		Black rape seed

NATURAL DYES

Have you ever noticed the colour of water after spinach has been cooked in it? Or the way that beetroot colours all the other foods on the plate? Why throw away all that bright colour when your child could trap it in fabric, wool, string or the shell of an egg? Boiling extracts colour from plant material: soft, subtle, earthy colours that never clash and are muted reminders of the richness of the plant material.

But remember, that to make a natural dye, you need mounds of plant material, often more than you think, so experiment carefully.

A country walk may produce fleece gathered from barbed-wire fences. This can be teased, spun and carded ready for dyeing. You can dye unbleached wool, string, unbleached calico, cotton or linen. Cotton and linen, however, require complicated mordanting (colour fixing) if colours are not to fade. The art-works children produce may not be subjected to washing, with the result that fading and running of colour can be avoided. For easy fixed colour, try using the plants that yield permanent colour, as shown on the chart.

PREPARING THE PLANTS

Wash and clean the plants to remove dirt and dead leaves. If you are using coffee beans or loose grains, tie them in an old stocking or piece of muslin and remember to use only white string – coloured string may shed its dye and influence the end result. Add the base material to water and bring to the boil. Simmer and stir from time to time until the colour has drained from the plants and the water is strongly coloured. If you have tied the ingredient in a stocking or muslin, squeeze it occasionally with a pair of tongs during boiling.

Use a large enamel pot as certain metals affect the colours. A big stick should be used for stirring and lifting: and remember to wear rubber gloves.

When the dye is ready, let it cool and strain the liquid through a handy colander, strainer or cheesecloth.

FIXING THE COLOUR

Traditionally, this fixing process is carried out before the dyeing. For 450 g (1 lb) fabric weight, allow 25 g (1 oz) cream of tartar, and 100 g (3½ oz) of alum. Dissolve the alum and the cream of tartar in a little water and add it to 11 litres (2½ gals) of water. Wetted fabric is added to this mix, and the liquid brought slowly to the boil, then simmered for 45 minutes. Then fabric is removed and drained. It is now ready to be dyed in the strained dye liquid you have prepared.

However, for speedier work with impatient young helpers, simply add the alum and the cream of tartar (same proportions) to the dye liquor. Then add wetted fabric and stir and lift the fabric in the dye while boiling for at least 30 minutes. Certain combinations of colour and fabric will take an hour or more. Leave to cool in the dye for stronger colour, rinse and hang to dry.

NATURAL DYE COLOURS

Colours derived from natural materials will always vary according to the season, moisture content of the plant and quantity used. This list is a guide to colours that you can expect the plants to yield, but experiment and experience are the two ingredients needed for certainty.

BEIGE Dock
       Heather

BLUE Blackberries
      Privet berries (bluish green)

BROWN Bracken
       Ground coffee
       Oak bark
       Tea leaves
       Walnut husks and shells

GREEN Alder catkins
       Bracken buds
       Goldenrod
       Privet berries (bluish green)
       Privet leaves
       Rhododendron leaves
       Spinach
       Tomato leaves
       Wild onion grass

PINK Madder

PURPLE Birch bark
        Elderberries (fresh)
        Marjoram flowerbuds
        Sorrel

YELLOW Birch bark (yellow gold)
        Birch leaves
        Dandelion flower heads
        Dog's mercury
        Elder leaves
        Goldenrod
        Heather (mustard yellow)
        Marigold petals
        Onion skins (yellow to ochre)
        Pine cones (reddish yellow-ochre)
        Ragwort
        Stinging nettles
        Weld
        Young bracken (greenish yellow)

SELF-FIXING COLOURS

The following are self-fixing colours. They require no mordant.

BROWN Bracken (sometimes light green)
       Oak acorns and bark
         (brownish black)
       Walnut husks (July–Oct)

GREEN Alder catkins
       Bracken (sometimes brown)
       Goldenrod (yellowish green)

PINK/
PURPLE Bilberry berries

RED Alder bark

YELLOW Alder (young shoots)
        Goldenrod (yellow gold –
          sometimes greenish)
        Heather (July-Sept) (golden yellow)
        Weld

TIE AND DYE

An ancient yet ageless craft, the tie and dye method can be used on paper or fabric to produce unusual and exotic designs with your natural dyes. The idea is to create an area that is so tightly knotted, twisted, clipped or bound, that it resists the dye. Attractive repeat patterns result when the fabric is first folded, then bound. Successive colours can be used, the article being rinsed, dried and sometimes re-tied before the dyeing process is repeated.

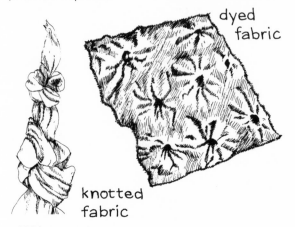

dyed
fabric

knotted
fabric

With young children, cotton fabrics are easy to work with and they should be well washed and ironed first. Suitable papers include absorbent kitchen towel, paper napkins, tissue papers, wallpaper and shelving paper amongst many. Experiment with twisting, rolling, folding and binding techniques to see the various patterns they make. Vary your 'tying'; binding fabric around other objects, like clumps of seeds or pebbles, pleating around a popsicle stick, umbrella fashion, or folding many times and securing with a spring clip. Stitching and gathering can be tried, accordion pleats, rope-like coils and squares folded again and again are a few suggestions. Save string, rubber bands, raffia, pipecleaners, clips, pegs and grips for reuse.

The peaked points sticking up from knots can always be dipped in another dye as an accent, or certain folded edges dyed with a brush for detailed patterns.

EASTER EGGS

Many countries boast traditional designs for gloriously decorative Easter eggs using techniques as diverse as découpage, in which shapes and designs are applied to the egg, or simple string collage, in which the string is glued onto the egg in whorls or zigzags, then varnished. Children of all ages enjoy decorating eggs. The easiest way is with a felt tip pen, but why not try the wax resist and dye method?

Draw on eggs with a mixture of equal parts of beeswax and paraffin wax. Then steep them in a dye bath made from some of the suggestions on this page.

The wax-and-dye process can be repeated on the same egg to build up layers of colour and a more intricate design. Use the lighter colours first, making the dye-bath darker as you go on. New designs are drawn on in wax before each dyeing. Wax left on from earlier dyes will resist colour. When the design is complete, the egg can be cleaned by heating it gently and wiping off the wax with an absorbent paper towel. This job takes longer than seems likely, so seek out a very patient volunteer.

Faces, patterns, geometrics, animals and abstracts will all feature in these imaginative and appealing decorations.

Older children can use fragile hollowed out eggs. To hollow out an egg, pierce each end with a needle. Enlarge one of the holes and blow through the smaller one until the contents of the egg come through the larger hole, then wash and dry. Younger children may be happier with eggs hard-boiled for 30 minutes. Hollowed-out eggs have the advantage that a 'masterpiece' can be kept for a long time. Hard-boiled eggs go off.

useful
patterns
for
Easter eggs

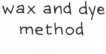

wax and dye
method

felt pen

Colour your Easter eggs with these plant dyes

BLACK	Alder bark
BLUE	Blackberries Privet berries
BROWN	Alder bark (long steep) Coffee Onion peel (longer steep than for yellow) Tea
GREEN	Nettle roots and leaves Rhododendron leaves Spinach
PURPLE	Elderberries (fresh) Marjoram flowerbuds Pink and red sorrel
RED	Beetroot juice Onion peel and vinegar
YELLOW	Alder bark Caraway seed Dandelion flowerheads Goldenrod Marigold petals Onion peel (short steep) Saffron

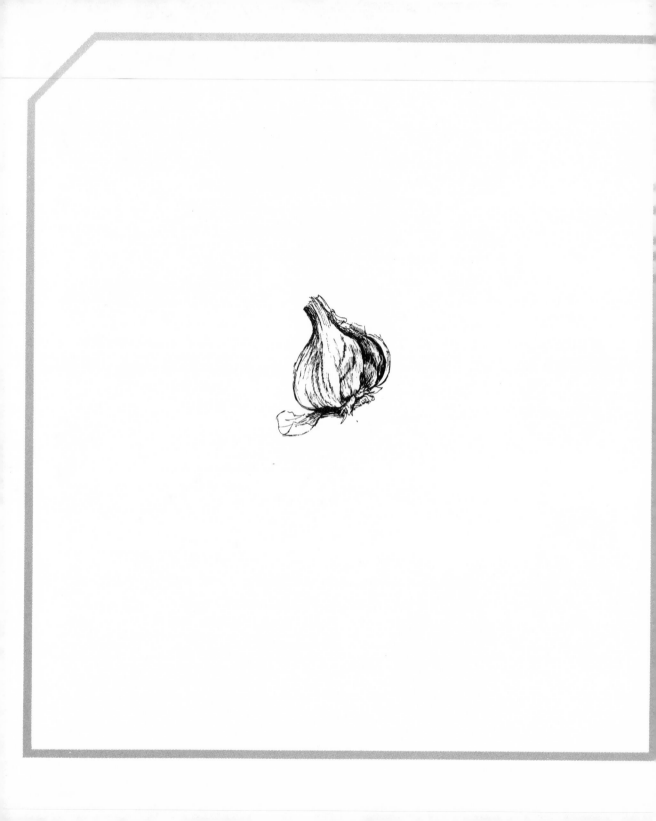

PLANT MAGIC

Mucilaginous Anodyne Liquor

'Of quick snails, newly taken out of their
shelly cottages, of Elderberries dried in the
oven; and pulverized; and of common salt,
of each as much as you will, put in the
straining bagg, called Hippocrates' sleeve,
making one row upon another, so oft as
you please; so that the first be of snails, the
next of salt and the last of berries,
continuing so till the bagg be full; hang it up
in the cellar, and gather diligently the
glutinous liquid that distils out of it – little by
little.'

Antomica Sambuco (or *The anatome of the Elder*)
Martin Blochwich

MAGICAL HERBS

bay

rosemary

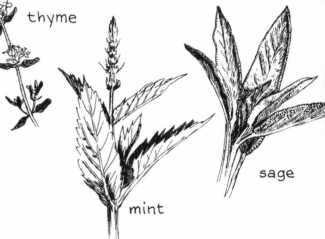

thyme

mint

sage

Gather the herbs and flowers from your garden or countryside: buy them: or grow them in your window box: but always pick from healthy, fully mature plants, and when a few flowers are beginning to come out. A dry sunny day is ideal picking weather, for the plants should not have much moisture on them. Plants picked from a verge or other roadside site are probably covered with fumes from traffic. To be useful, they must be free of pollution, chemicals and insecticides. Pick them gently, making sure that they are not squeezed in hot, little hands and lay them gently on paper. If they are perfectly clean there is no need to wash them – but, if in doubt, rinse them. Spread them in a thin layer and dry out in an airy, shady spot. Have children turn them from time to time.

As 'quick snails' don't hang around in our gardens these days, we can't fortunately testify to the powers of Martin Blochwich's brew, but for centuries, plants, and especially herbs, have been invested with magic powers and there are many herbal recipes that are easy to make and that do work. Several of them are useful for common gardening ailments – tired and aching feet or rough, chapped hands.

Many plants have medicinal and beautifying powers and enthusiasts might like to dip into one of the many excellent herbals to develop a repertoire of herbal remedies.

I have included here only a handful of recipes that are easy for children to prepare, using herbs that are generally available.

First things first

When gathering herbs, take great care that the plants picked have been correctly identified. A field guide is essential to make certain that neither you nor your child confuse dangerous plants.

When dried, cut them up or let your young helpers rub them between their hands to detach the leaves, and then letting them smell the herbs on their fingers store them in glass jars in a dark cupboard. Roots should be cut up and dried in a slow oven and some will need to be powdered or ground up later.

Fragrant freezing

Herbs can be frozen in ice cubes. Cut the herbs or strip the leaves off into a little water and freeze in a block, ready for use. A teaspoon of herbs per block is about right.

USES FOR SOME HERBS AND PLANTS

Children may be fascinated to learn that Roman soldiers were given cloves of garlic while on the march to strengthen them up. Even labourers in ancient Egypt were given a daily dose of garlic to keep them up to

scratch. So if you want to get the best out of your little helpers you know what to do...

The sand-paper-like texture of many plants of the Horsetail family has been used traditionally for polishing and scouring. Medieval bow-and-arrow makers used these plants to smooth the shafts of their arrows. The stems bunched together will make an effective scouring tool – a little like steel wool. If this is dipped in a little cranberry juice it makes a sparkling silver cleaner.

Sphagnum moss has long been gathered from the wild to dress wounds received in battle. The plant is highly absorbent, rather like a super breed of cotton wool. Its antiseptic qualities and preservative phenols add to its medical attractions and even today it is used, dried and sterilized, for packing dressings.

The smell of elder leaves will keep flies at bay, so on a picnic or when barbecuing wear a sprig in your hair.

A HERBAL TALCUM IS ALWAYS WELCOME

Soothe gardeners' aching feet with this easy-to-make powder that's also acceptable as a gift for a gardening granny. Spells chanted while you're mixing the ingredients weave their special magic.

Method
Mix equal amounts of Fuller's Earth and some dried powdered elder leaves. Instant relief when sprinkled in shoes or gumboots.

Store it in a glass jar with a stopper which can be decorated with a pretty ribbon tied round the neck.

A BATH FOR TIRED FEET

While on the subject of these tired feet, try a refreshing footbath. You'll enjoy having one with a couple of marbles thrown into the bowl for tired toes to twiddle.

Method
Put one tablespoonful of leaves (a mixture of rosemary and mint, or marigold on its own) into a footbath or washing up bowl. Ask an adult to pour in about 2 litres (4½ pints) of boiling water. Leave to steep for about fifteen minutes, strain and while still warm, stick your feet into it.

BAGS OF DELIGHT

Children enjoy making simple and easy muslin bags with long ties that can be hung in the bath. These have blends of herbs inside them to scent the water, healing, soothing, cooling, softening – ideal restoratives for harassed parents. Check that the bags are tightly stitched, or the bath may look like a fortune-teller's tea-cup when the water has drained away.

Experiment with soothing and refreshing peppermint, deodorizing lovage, skin-softening elder leaves or flowers and invigorating pine needles to concoct your favourite blend.

SWEET-SMELLING WATERS

Keep an eye out for lovely, old stoppered bottles which are perfect for bottling herbal scented waters to be added to bath-water or sprinkled wherever you want a natural, fresh perfume, on a handkerchief or clothing. Use as a handy refresher after slogging it out in the garden or give a friend a bottle of violet water.

Ask your young helpers to gather enough of the chosen herb to fill a half-litre (1 pint) jug. Then ask them to make attractive labels and to select appropriate ribbons to tie around the necks – the bottles' not the kids' (though you may occasionally feel this way)! While they're happily occupied pour on enough water to fill the jug and leave to cool. Then, pour it into the bottles.

Try violet, thyme, bergamot or lemon balm and ignore little boys who say, 'You stink!'

BRUISE BALM

Do you have the sort of child whose body looks like soft fruit that has been dropped from a great height? A bruised battlefield? Falling out of trees every day and the usual daily dose of the sprains and bashes of childhood result in aches and bruises. Try some St John's Wort Oil to treat your sorry soldier.

Method
Put 50 grammes (2 oz) of St John's Wort leaves in a screw-top jar along with 300 millilitres (½ pint) of pure sunflower oil and a tablespoonful of wine vinegar. Put the lid on tightly and stand it on a sunny window ledge for 4–5 weeks. Remind your child to give the bottle of magic potion a good shake every day (make sure it's a tight-fitting cap) and ask him to design a purple and yellow label for the bruise balm.

This is also helpful for sunburn.

HAND SOFTENING CREAM

Rough sore hands can be restored to softness with buttercup cream made by warming 250 grams (8 oz) of Vaseline in an old pan over a low heat with as many buttercup heads as you need to cover the Vaseline. Make sure that you don't boil the mixture, but simmer it very slowly for 45 minutes: then strain it into jars to set.

HERB SACHETS

Scraps of pretty fine lawn or muslin can be simply stitched together into small bags which children can fill with herbs. These can be slipped into clothes-cupboards and boxes of writing paper spreading a whiff of lavender or rose petals. I like a combination of lemon verbena and lavender fixed with strips of dried citrus peel or cinnamon.

HEADACHE CUSHION

An angelic child will offer you this when you snap, 'Shut up! Can't you see I've got a headache!'

Make a cushion-size bag of muslin or fine cotton lawn and fill it with equal amounts of peppermint and spearmint. Add a few drops of eau de Cologne with a little bergamot and a tablespoonful of powdered orris root to act as a fixative.

KEEP THE MOTHS AT BAY

The smell of mothballs lingers on clothes even after they've been aired, so try keeping moths at bay and give some garments a pleasant aroma at the same time with these moth bags. Gather a selection of thyme, rosemary, sage, sweet marjoram, lavender or mint and combine them together with some powdered orris root or crushed cinnamon. (Mint and rosemary are powerful enough to be used on their own.) Put the herbs into little sachets, sew them closed and attach a ribbon. The moths will stay away and your clothes will smell herb fresh.

A CAT AND MOUSE GAME

Cats are attracted by the smell of *Nepeta cataria* ... O.K. catmint. If you have it growing in your garden, gather a bunch and let it dry. Stuff some into a mouse-shaped bag made with fabric scraps ... your cat will have great fun with his new plaything.

POT-POURRI

Standing on my desk as I write is a delicate little ceramic bowl filled with pot-pourri, the scent wafting over to me every now and then, intense yet delicate, distinctive yet blended. Petals, leaves and herbs can be collected by children for this – there are many to choose from, but try to have one dominating perfume such as rose or lavender.

The petals and leaves must be carefully dried to preserve their colour and scent so that they will remain fragrant for a long time. You can add bulk and extra colour by using dry, brightly coloured flowers and buds – even those without much scent of their own. Include larkspur, marigolds, anchusa, grape hyacinth and the curry plant which does not retain its strong smell when dried.

A fixative of some kind must be added to pot-pourris to blend all the fragrances together and to retard the evaporation of essential oils which provide the scents. Powdered orris root, strips of citrus fruit peel, cinnamon and cloves are often used for this purpose. For every 2 litres (4 pints) of dried flowers you will need 110 grams (4 oz) of fixative.

Crushed or ground spices can also be added to the mixture. Choose from coriander, nutmeg, cloves, allspice and mace, and don't overlook anise or vanilla pods.

A few drops of essential oil (a condensed extract available at health and herb shops) will intensify the perfume but should be used with care, for too many drops will be overpowering. Try rosemary, geranium, lavender, rose, peppermint or bergamot oil.

Lay the flower petals out flat on a sheet of paper or a tray to dry in a warm place. Press some petals and leaves as they look attractive on the top of a pile of pot-pourri in a glass bowl.

Mix your chosen combination together and store in a tightly sealed glass jar for about five weeks to steep.

The traditional way of using pot-pourri for maximum effect was to keep the jars shut during the day, and, in the evening, the jars were set near the fire and gently warmed. The lids were removed and perfume released to waft around the room. Special stands were made to hold the jars as they cooled and finally the lid was closed tightly again. This method retained the perfume for many months.

Nothing beats letting the pot-pourri fall from the hand as you turn it occasionally in a large glass bowl and allow the aroma to float out.

AN EASY POT-POURRI

For a simple moist pot-pourri, find a large earthenware crock and put in a layer of rose petals, 10 centimetres (4 inches) deep. Then add a thin layer of common salt. Continue to add alternate layers of rose petals and salt until the jar is full. Cover and leave for about ten days in a dark, airy place. When the mixture has settled, break up the mixture with a wooden spoon and add dried orange peel, crushed clove and orris root. Blend them all together and leave, covered and sealed for six weeks, shaking frequently to keep it well mixed. Add a drop of essential oil if required and leave for another week or two. The pot-pourri is then ready to be put into small pottery jars.

BUNDLES OF LAVENDER

Making lavender bundles (or baskets) is peaceful work on a warm summer afternoon. Tie a ribbon around the bundle just under the heads. Now carefully bend the stalks back over the heads, until they form a sort of cage around the heads.

Secure with thread or an elastic band while yo[u] gently weave the ribbon, basket-weave style over and under the stalks. When you have wove[n] up to the elastic band, tie the ribbon tightly an[d] make a bow. The band can now be remove[d]. Trim the ends of the stalks neatly.

An alternative is to plait the stalks into [a] circular 'handle' for the basket, plaiting some ribbon in with the stalks.

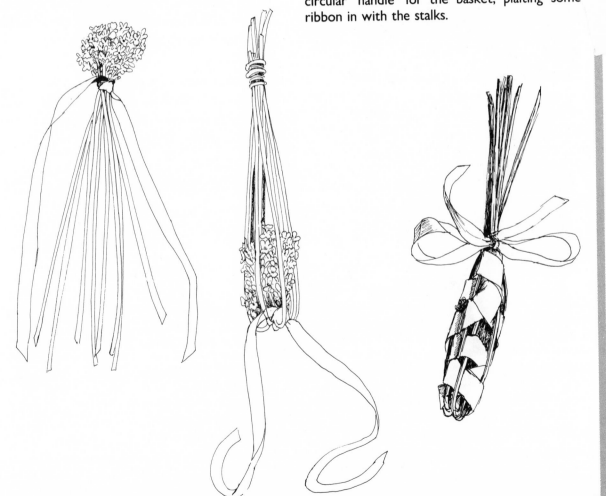

FLORAL CODES

Some plants and flowers have special associations and meaning. Here's a selection of some of the most popular.

Aconite – *crime*
Alyssum – *the power to allay anger*
Anemone – *foresaken*
Bluebell – *constancy*
Clematis – *spiritual beauty*
Cornflower – *delicacy*
Fern – *sincerity*
Forget-me-not – *true-love, constancy*
Helichrysums – *never forget*
Hellebore – *wit*
Iris – *a message*
Lily of the valley – *return of happiness*
Magnolia – *love of nature*

Mistletoe – *protection from evil spirits*
Nasturtium – *patriotism*
Orange lily – *hatred*
Pink carnations – *mother*
Ranunculus – *you are fascinating and attractive*
Red carnations – *admiration*
Red roses – *I love you*
White jasmine – *cheerfulness*
White lily – *sincerity and motherhood*
White roses – *you are charming*
Yellow jasmine – *timidity*
Yellow roses – *I am jealous*
Red roses to you all.

Can you decipher the iris?
Ranunculus in all fern. I feel red carnations for your hellebore and yellow roses of your white jasmine. Regarding your aconite, I hope you've got alyssum and mistletoe.

USEFUL LISTS

And he wrote it down . . . like this:

ORDER OF LOOKING FOR THINGS

1. Special Place   (To find Piglet)

2. Piglet   (To find out who Small is.)

3. Small   (To find Small.)

4. Rabbit   (To tell him I've found Small.)

5. Small Again   (To tell him I've found Rabbit.)

'Which makes it look like a bothering sort
of day', thought Pooh, as he stumped along.

The House at Pooh Corner A. A. Milne

NATURAL PEST CONTROL

SOME COMMON PESTS

Ants: If they are becoming too much of a pest, try sprinkling a mixture of an equal amount of borax and icing sugar in the infested area.

Derris is a safe pesticide, harmless to humans, that is readily available from most garden centres. It comes either as a dusting powder or a liquid and should be used in strict accordance with the instructions.

A simpler (and free) alternative is to pour a strong decoction of elder leaves over the ants' nests. This should dispose of them overnight.

Ants hate marigolds, tansy, chives and lavender. Clusters of these will leave these parts of the garden ant-free.

Aphids: These are simply dealt with by spraying with hot water at 12°C (54°F). Soap solution is effective, too. Another effective treatment is to spray with oxalic acid, obtainable from rhubarb leaves. Make an infusion of rhubarb leaves and add some soap flakes to it. Spray the infected plant, both upper and under surfaces of the leaves. Any surplus spray should be thrown away. Do not store the liquid once the soap flakes have been added.

Slugs and snails: Half-bury some saucers in the ground and fill them with beer. This method will also deal with other pests if you add brown sugar to the beer and mix this with an equal amount of water. Slugs and snails will not go near hyssop and thyme.

Woodlice and earwigs: Often found in greenhouses, they can be trapped in halved grapefruit or orange skins, turned upside down on the greenhouse staging. A scooped-out potato will trap woodlice and cucumber rinds can be used to capture earwigs.

SOME NON-TOXIC WAYS OF CONTROLLING PESTS

Pidero, a combination of pyrethrum (a safe, non-toxic derivitive from chrysanthemums) and derris, is effective against weevils, beetles, ants and millipedes among others.

Salt can be used as a weedkiller in paths. Sprinkle and leave dry for a few days.

Flour dusted on to both sides of leaves deters egg-laying insects.

Garlic interplanted with other crops will cut down attack by insects. They find the smell intolerable. Onions will have the same effect. Sprays can be made by mincing 2 cloves of garlic, 1 large onion and 2 hot peppers very finely and mixing in 2 cups of hot water. Infuse for 2 hours, strain and sprinkle the mushy mix between the crops. Essential oil of garlic is also efficient against aphids, cabbage white butterflies and Colorado beetle.

Herbs contain volatile oils that act as repellents, so interplant them in other parts of the garden. Chives, coriander, sage and savory can be used in infusions and sprayed onto plants.

Nettles can be soaked in water (450 grams [1 lb] of leaves in 4.5 litres [1 gallon] of water) for a couple of days and used as a food for bulbs. It builds up their resistance to insects and disease.

...NG POISONS

...ome-made or natural remedies or
...onous. Mark them as poison and
..., best of all, make up the amount
...store any left-overs. Dispose of
...tain you do not bottle these
...ottles or other bottles a child
...for.

Nicotine is a poison, but 100 grams (4 oz) of tobacco boiled in 4.5 litres (1 gallon) of water, then cooled and strained will eradicate caterpillars, aphids, weevils, cabbage whites and leaf miners. If you are storing the solution, label the bottle 'Poison': and never apply within a month of harvesting crops.

Caustic soda is a useful insecticide for use against red spider, mealy bug, apple sucker, aphids, weevils, wintermoth and fungi. 350 grams (12 oz) soda and 225 grams (8 oz) of soap dissolved in 27 litres (8 gallons) of water is the best mix. Make sure that you are wearing rubber gloves before adding the soda to the water, and then put the soap in. Keep the mixture away from children.

Careless use of chemical fertilizers can kill bees and other day-time, beneficial visitors to your garden. Best spray at night with a short-term acting remedy when these creatures are no longer about (Pyrethrum is effective for short periods).

AMERICAN PLANTS THAT ARE POISONOUS

Autumn Crocus (*Colchicum autumnale*)
Black Henbane (*Hyoscyamus niger*)
Brazilian Pepper (*Schinus terebinthifolius*)
Castor Bean (*Ricinus communis*)
Daffodil (*Narcissus* spp.)
Deadly nightshade (*Solanum americanum* and *S. nigrum*)
Dumb Cane (*Dieffenbachia* spp.)
Foxglove (*Digitalis purpurea*)
Horse Chestnut (*Aesculus* spp.)
Ivy (*Hedera helix*)
Jerusalem cherry (*Solanum pseudo-capsicum*)
Jack-in-the-pulpit (*Arisaema triphyllum*)
Jimsonweed (*Datura stramonium*)
Lily-of-the-valley (*Convallaria majalis*)
Lupines (*Lupinus* spp.)
May Apple (*Podophyllum peltatum*)
Marijuana (*Cannabis sativa*)
Matrimony vine (*Lycium halimifolium*)
Milkweeds (*Asclepias* spp.)
Mistletoe (*Phoradendron* spp.)
Monkshood (*Aconitum* spp.)
Morning Glory (*Convolvulus* spp.)
Oleander (*Nerium oleander*)
Opium poppy (*Papaver somniferum*)
Pencil Tree Cactus (*Euphorbia tirucalli*)
Poison hemlock (*Conium maculatum*)
Poison Ivy (*Toxicodendron radicans*)
Poison Oak (*Toxicodendron diversilobum* and *T. toxicarium*)
Poison Sumac (*Toxicodendron vernix*)
Poisonwood (*Metopium toxiferum*)
Pokeweed (*Phytolacca americana*)
Precatory bean (*Abrus precatorius*)
Rhubarb (*Rheum ponticum*)
Stinging Nettles (*Urtica dioica*)
Yew (*Taxus baccata*)
Fungi should be left alone unless you really know what you are picking

Ageratum: pink and blue forms: compact forms 15–23cm (6–9in) high, taller ones available

Althaea rosea (Hollyhock): look for doubles

Antirrhinum majus (Snapdragon): self seeding

Begonia fibrous: ever flowering; bronze- or green-leaved

Begonia tuberous: showy flowers

Bellis perennis (Double daisy): neat for edging

Calendula officinalis (Pot marigold): the common name comes from the old custom of boiling marigolds in a pot to be used as a cure for toothache, spots and warts in medieval times. Ideal for children.

Callistephus chinensis (China aster): from dwarf varieties to 76cm (2ft 4in) Californian giants

Campanula medium (Canterbury bell): stately, tall spikes of bell-like flowers

Centaurea cyanus (Cornflower): old, well-loved hardy annual

Chrysanthemum carinatum: showy and hardy

Clarkia elegans: tall and spiky

Coleus blumei: colourful foliage: looks hand-painted

Consolida ambigua (Rocket larkspur): mauve to blue spikes

Coreopsis grandiflora (Tickseed): will tolerate pollution

Dahlia pinnata: colourful bedding plants

Dianthus barbatus (Sweet William): these showy plants can be grown as a perennial in some areas

Dianthus chinensis (Indian pink): compact and colourful

Digitalis purpurea (Common foxglove): graceful spikes of bells. **Poisonous.**

Echium lycopsis: adaptable

Eschscholzia californica (Poppy): brilliant silky cups

Helianthus annuus (Sunflower): gigantic and cheerful with edible seeds

Gypsophila elegans (Baby's breath): white froth.

Iberis umbellata (Candytuft): easy; compact; pink, white and lavender

Impatiens walleriana (Busy Lizzie): will grow in light shade. Grow from cuttings.

Lathyrus odoratus (Sweet pea): lovely to look at with heady perfume. Cut flowers.

Lavatera trimestis (Mallow): self sowing

Limpanthes douglasii (Poached-egg plant): their nectar is beloved of insects

Linaria maroccana (Moroccan toadflax): upright, delicate plants with bright colours

Linum grandiflora (Flax): sow successively

Lobelia crinus: well known in blue, now in pink and white forms. Trailing or upright.

Lobularia maritima (Sweet alyssum): self-sowing in cracks and beds

Lupinus hartweggii (Lupin): glorious spikes of colour

Malcomia maritima (Virginia stock): broadcast freely

Matthiola bicornis: easy annual; strongest perfume of any stock

Matthiola incana: perfumed spikes in soft grey foliage

Myosotis sylvatica (Forget-me-not): seeds freely

Nemesia strumosa: masses of blooms in varied colours

Nemophilia menziesii (Baby blue eyes): trailing mound of blue. Easy.

Nicotiana alata (Tobacco plant): heady perfume nightly

Nigella damascena (Love-in-a-mist): though delicate in form, hardy and easy

Papaver rhoeas (Field poppy): throw a patch of seed into a wild corner

Penstemon x gloxinoides: tall, robust spikes of bells. Good cut flowers. Perennial in some areas.

Petunia x hybrida: ever popular half hardy annual; ideal in pots. Likes sunny spots and well-drained soil.

Phlox drummondii: compact plants with clustered flowers. Soft tones with bright 'eyes'. Dead head to prolong flowering.

Portulaca grandiflora (Sun plant): in sunshine these reward with glowing colour borne on spreading mats. Little care needed.

Reseda odorata (Mignonette): successive sowings will give prolonged unique fragrance in the garden or in a window box

Ricinus communis (Castor oil plant): seeds are used to produce castor oil but this plant is grown for its quick effect and showy foliage. Bronze forms available.

Salpiglossis sinuata: tall, needs support; a profusion of fiery shades

Salvia farinacea: this is the delicate purple/blue variety and is not a spaghetti plant! The name derives from the light dusting of farina covering stems and leaves.

Salvia splendens: bright bedding plant

Scabiosa atropurpurea (Sweet scabious): tall and delicate with pom-pom-like heads

Schizanthus pinnatus (Butterfly flower): orchid-like, tiny flowers cluster together with fern-like foliage. Short flowering season; dwarfs best as summer annuals.

Tagetes erecta (African marigold): taller than the French marigolds with large round heads. Strong aroma.

Tagetes patula (French marigolds): bushy, short, compact and showy. Easy.

Thunbergia alata (Black-eyed Susan): in sunny corners on strings will climb and form a yellow column

Tropaeolum majus (Nasturtium): trailing and vivid; thrives in poor soil.

Ursinias: happy in poor soil; produces a glow of yellow daisy heads

Verbena x hybrida: most are bushy. Sparkle Mixed is a trailer. Clusters of flowers; long flowering.

Viola x wittrockiana (Garden pansies): biennial or annual; successive sowing will produce colour for many months. Dead head vigorously.

Zinnia elegans: dislikes root disturbance; sow where to flower

PLANTS FOR BALCONY OR PATIO

Plan a permanent framework of small trees and shrubs which are happy in containers. This overall design is then filled with perennials and annuals using many of the examples listed for window boxes on page 126. In a tiny space each plant has greater weight in the design, so its beauty, neat form or perfume must recommend it.

Evergreen

Laurel (bay laurel), Camellias, Cotoneaster, Chinese Fan Palm, Box (buxus), Hollies (Ilex), Berberis, Hebes, Hypericum, and of course the dwarf conifers, Junipers, *Juniperus chinensis* 'Pyramidalis', a blue form, and *Juniperus Sabina tamariscifolia* which is prostrate; the dwarf cypresses (*C. Lawsoniana* 'Elswoodii') form a background.

Deciduous

Look at small Japanese maples (*Acer palmatum*), Artopurpurea, for a glorious autumn show. Azaleas too turn reddish in autumn and are so prolific when flowering; Fuchsias, Hydrangeas, Roses, climbing and standard, Chaenomeles, Blue spiraeas, Caryopteris, Ceratostigma, Potentillas and small Citrus trees.

Some particularly strong shapes are found amongst Hostas, *Phormium tenax*, Bergenias, *Centaurea dealbata*, Sedums and Acanthus; lovely foliage too from Anchusa, Dicentra and Achillea.

Ivies may be grown to cover unsightly features, clipped and trained or simply allowed to ramble over paving.

WINDOW BOX GARDENING

A taller group for height at the back

Annual climbers (Black-eyed Susan, Ipomoea etc.)

Green beans

Junipers

Passiflora

Shrubby veronicas

Plants for the middle tier

Ageratum

Antirrhinum (dwarf forms – Snapdragon)

Begonia semperflorens

Busy Lizzie (*Impatiens*)

Celosia plumosa (dwarf forms – Fairy fountain and Lilliput)

Chrysanthemums (dwarf forms)

Campanulas (fairies' thimbles)

Dianthus

Forget-me-not

Geraniums (Pelargoniums)

Godetia varieties

Iberis umbellata (dwarf Candytuft)

Linarias

Marguerites

Marigolds (dwarf French)

Matricaria

Nasturtiums (dwarf)

Nemesia hybrids

Nicotiana

Pansies

Petunias

Phlox drummondii

Roses (miniature)

Salvias

Schizanthus (Poor man's orchid)

Senecio

Sweetpeas (dwarf)

Sweet William (dwarf)

Verbena

Wallflowers

Zinnias (dwarf, Peter Pan)

Trailing plants to hang down over the edge of the window box

Alyssum (grows in crevices and will spill over the edge)

Arabis (pink or white)

Aubretia (purple Rock cress)

Campanula (some forms)

Cerastium tomentosum (Snow-in-summer; silver leaves in a dense mat; white flowers)

Fuchsia

Geraniums (ivy-leafed)

Helichrysum petiolatum (for foliage)

Ivies

Lobelia (dark or light blue; sometimes pink or white)

Lysimachia (Creeping Jenny – masses of yellow flowers)

Nasturtium (*Tropaeolum majus*)

Petunias

Phlox subulata

Woolly thyme

Zebrina

DRYING FLOWERS

Plants suited to air drying

Agapanthus seed heads

Alchemilla

Allium seed heads

Artichoke

Ballota

Berries

Bouganvillea

Bracken

Celosia

Centaurea

Chinese lanterns (Cape gooseberry)

Clematis seed heads

Cockscomb

Corn

Delphinium seed heads

Dock

Eryngium (Sea holly)

Eucalyptus leaves

Everlastings

Ferns

Globe thistle

Goldenrod

Gypsophila

Heathers

Helichrysum

Hollyhock seed heads

Honesty seeds

Hops and grasses

Hydrangea (place the stems in a little water and leave to dry)

Lupines

Okra

Pampas grass

Pine cones

Pods

Poppyseed pods

Rose hips

Sorrel seeds

Statice (Limonium or Sea lavender)

Tansy

Teazle

Wheat and barley

In glycerine

Gather sprays of leaves in dry, warm weather. Hammer the ends of the stems.

Aspidistra

Beech

Eleagnus

Horse chestnut

Laurel

Magnolia

Sweet chestnut

Plants suited to sand drying

Camellias

Carnations

Cornflowers

Daffodils

Delphiniums

Dogwood

Feverfew

Hyacinth

Larkspur

Lilacs

Marigolds

Peonies

Pointsettia

Roses

Scabious

Zinnias

INDEX

Acknowledgements

For the inclusion of copyright material, the publishers gratefully acknowledge the following:

p9: by permission of Barry Maybury and taken from his *Wordspinners* published by Oxford University Press, 1981
p10: © Ogden Nash, reproduced on behalf of the estate of Ogden Nash by Curtis Brown Limited, London, and taken from *Collected Poems of Ogden Nash* published by J M Dent & Sons Limited, 1961
p33: by permission of Mrs Richmal Ashbee and taken from *Just William* published by Fontana, 1972
p69: by kind permission of David Higham Associates and published by Chatto & Windus Limited, 1975
p83: © Charles Tomlinson 1978, reprinted from his *Selected Poems 1951–1974*, and by permission of Oxford University Press, published 1978